Stewarts Ri\

By Hamisl

CW00508134

Stewarts River Revenge by Hamish McBain Published Internationally by Marvin Press – PO Box 14, Cundletown, NSW, 2430, Australia.

Copyright Marvin Press 2017

All rights reserved. The purchaser of this book is subject to the condition that he/she shall in no way resell it, nor any part of it, nor make copies of it or portions thereof in any form whatsoever.

This book is a work of fiction. Any similarity between the characters and situations within its pages and places or persons, living or dead, is unintentional and co-incidental.

Chapter 1

Mick Gallagher was pulled from deep sleep by the incessant ringing of the "On Call" phone. His arm clumsily reached from under the sheets towards the bedside table. Empty coffee cups clunked against empty beer bottles as he fumbled for the phone in the dark. Where the hell was it? Eventually his fingers found the vibrating phone and as he squinted at the luminous display it stated that it was 02:24. Bloody hell. He'd only been in bed 2 hours. He hit the answer key.

"Hello – This is Mick Gallagher from Stewarts River Veterinary Hospital...."

As his brain tried to kick into gear he hoped that this call would be a small animal call where with minimal effort he could be back in bed very soon, or even better fob any work off till breakfast time. The agitated voice on the other end of the phone had him wide awake and feeling sick in the guts within seconds. The heavy Greek accent was recognisable immediately.

"Mick – it's Joe Papantoniou from Athena Stud. We need you straight away. We've just unloaded our new stallion off the truck and he's gone through a fence and staked himself in the groin – there's blood pissing everywhere – it's spraying like a fire hose... He's worth millions... He's lost so much blood... You need to come right now... We flew him in from the Emirates 3 days ago. We need you right now. He's bleeding to death, Mick. You've got to come quickly..."

Mick felt nauseous. His brain was having problems comprehending the situation, or more likely, did not want to comprehend the situation.

"Mick... Are you there? He's bleeding to death Mick. You've got to come straight away..."Joe's voice was almost screaming.

The details that Mick had just been given were sinking in. They painted a dire scene and a veterinary nightmare. Five or six hundred kilos of very pissed off Arab stallion with a possible torn femoral artery or vein. The horse could be very dead within a few minutes. The situation would be very difficult to deal with at an equine hospital facility with multiple vets available, dedicated anaesthetists, nurses, handlers and support staff. They might have a chance if they could deal with it immediately. They would have sterile surgical facilities, with hoists and slings to lift the animal onto a padded surgical table and to position the horse in an ideal position for surgery. They would have state of the art surgical lights to illuminate the trauma site. If they were lucky and the planets were aligned... Maybe they would have a chance. Mick was 25-30minutes away. The horse was bleeding now. It could be dead in 3-4 minutes. If he got there and the horse was still alive would he only be going to give the last rites? Would it be too far gone? The facilities were mediocre at best. Bare dirt under dirty bare light bulbs. No sterile facility there. The owner and his sidekicks were all in their sixties and seventies. Could they even hold the animal, never mind assist with a procedure? Mick would be anaesthetist, surgeon and nurse all on his own. This could be an absolute nightmare. Mick's brain was screaming silently but his voice was clear and calm.

"OK Joe – I'll be there as fast as I can...But until I get there you need to apply pressure to the wound...and I mean real pressure... Strap towels or a pillow to the wound as tightly as you can....If he's hit the femoral artery or vein he could bleed out in minutes."

"But he'll try and kick the shit out of us..."

"Joe – if he continues to bleed – he could be dead before I get there"

"OK, OK we'll try – Get here fast"

"I'm on my way"

As Mick hung up the phone he was already climbing into overalls and heading for his truck. This was a hellish callout that he wouldn't wish on anyone else. But why the hell did he have to get the job? Shit. Fucking shit. This was going to be a bastard of a job... If the horse survived long enough for him to get there.

The stud was over thirty kilometres away, and more than twenty kilometres of that on dirt roads. He was going to have to fly. He jumped into the battered Holden Rodeo and gunned the engine. He burned rubber on the tarmac as he turned onto the highway out the front of the Vet Hospital and aimed north. Within a few seconds he was travelling at 120km/hr and still accelerating. He had a dull nauseous ache in the pit of his stomach, and in his mind's eye he could see a hysterical horse throwing itself around on the ground with fountains of blood spraying everywhere.

Fuck.... Fuck.....

After a minute or so he had crossed the Rankin Bridge and was hurtling towards town. A hundred metres short of the "Welcome to Stewarts River" sign Mick slowed and took a left. The Rodeo immediately accelerated again and rocketed west. After three more kilometres the vehicle left the bitumen behind and flew over red dirt roads leaving choking dust clouds swirling in its wake. Pot holes and corrugations jarred the vehicle every inch of the way but Mick barely noticed them. He was focused on travelling fast and not missing turn-offs. There was no room for getting lost tonight. He had to get to Athena Stud faster than ever before.

A full moon lit the night sky. The country was flat and stark, punctuated by skeletal moon shadows of large ghost gums and long fence lines. Cattle grids rattled painfully as the speeding vehicle hammered across them. Mobs of silhouetted kangaroos grazed on precious pasture oblivious to the unfolding drama. There were hundreds of them. When they moved en masse it appeared as if the earth itself was moving. Mick was oblivious to them. All he could see was a thrashing horse lying in a sea of blood.

Chapter 2

Seventeen minutes after receiving the call the Rodeo screeched to a halt in front of the floodlit round yard at Athena Stud. As Mick jumped out he was greeted by an ashen faced Joe Papantoniou.

"He's shocking Mick – can hardly stay on his feet – he's lost gallons of blood"

Mick ran straight past Joe and into the round yard to assess the situation for himself. Two figures were leaning into a huge black horse. One was holding the horse's head stall and leaning hard under his shoulder. The other had his arms wrapped around a mass of blood soaked towels and bandages strapped to the medial thigh of the horse's right hind leg. There was a constant trickle of blood through his fingers and into the sawdust on the ground. The whole yard was awash with red blood sitting in small puddles in the sawdust. The sawdust was the colour of red wine.

Mick recognised the two figures as Jake and Pete - Joe's regular offsiders. They both looked exhausted and pale. Pete the human tourniquet looked like he was crying and muttering expletives between clenched teeth. Jake stared at Mick with desperate, tortured eyes.

Mick checked the horse's vitals quickly. The mucous membranes of his gums were extremely pale – marginally pinker than white. He pulled a stethoscope from his pocket and auscultated the horses heaving chest. His heart rate was through the roof - 120 beats per minute. Normal would be 25-30/minute for a fit 500kg stallion. The horse was cold to the touch, sweating and shivering. His skin was turgid and tented markedly when Mick pinched it with his fingers. This indicated gross dehydration, likely associated with the severe blood loss. He was also weaving from side to side on his feet, threatening to crush Jake and Pete if he collapsed.

Mick directed his question to Pete.

"I assume that when the bandage is released or slackened off blood just gushes out?"

Pete nodded gravely.

"OK. Bear with me two more minutes. We're going to knock him out and tie off the torn blood vessels."

Mike raced back to the Rodeo and returned with a couple of large fishing tackle boxes full of drugs, syringes, needles and a couple of sterilised surgical kits. While filling syringes he gave all three – Joe, Jake, and Pete – precise instructions on his game plan.

"Jake. You stay on his head."

"I'm going to put a catheter in his jugular vein and then give him two injections to knock him out. One after the other."

"Now Jake – when he goes down – push him so that the bad leg is the one underneath – we need him on his right side."

"Pete, hold onto that bandage until you feel him going down and then get out of the way quick. Once he's on his side I need you lean over his back and put as much pressure back on the bandage as you can. You can actually lie on him if you want. You'll probably be more comfortable lying across him. Be careful he doesn't give you a boot with the other leg when you bend over him. If you stay on that side you're less likely to get kicked and it'll give me more room to work on the other side between his legs. He could be a little bit "light" when we first get started, but then he should settle down over a minute or two."

"Joe, we need you to put a lead rope around his left hind leg and pull it back out of the way, so that we have good access to the wound on the bad leg."

"We'll have about 20 minutes anaesthesia before he wakes. I might have to top him up as we go. We'll see."

"Pete, you're the main man. When we remove your bandage the blood will piss everywhere... I'll need you to push on the blood vessels above and below the wound to stop the bleeding while I explore and tie off the blood vessels. You may have to apply a shit load of pressure."

Pete looked even more ashen than previously.

"You'll be fine Pete. You just have to do it."

"Sterility will have to wait. We have to tie off the blood vessels before he bleeds to death. We'll worry about sterility and infection later."

There were no comments at all from any of the three. All eyes stared painfully at Mick. All looked knackered and sick.

Mick's mind was racing. This was a shocking scenario. If he did not stop the bleeding straight away the horse would be dead in minutes. It had lost a ridiculous amount of blood. Even if he managed to stop the bleeding it could still die. Performing general anaesthesia would have huge risks with the gross blood loss, but there was no way he could attempt to ligate major blood vessels with the horse conscious and likely to collapse at any moment. He was caught between the devil and the deep blue sea. Damned if he did, and worse damned if he didn't. He had to keep his composure and stick to his plan. He thought he might vomit.

Joe Papantoniou looked as if a coronary was on the cards. Jake was imploring the horse to stay upright. Pete's skinny arms were lost in the blood stained towels. He continued to swear and curse to no-one in particular... Or was he now talking to God?

Mick could do with help from anywhere. Divine intervention would be greatly appreciated.

Chapter 3

Finding the stallion's jugular vein was not easy as his blood pressure was ridiculously low, but within a few seconds the catheter was in place.

Mick slowly delivered a moderate dose of Xylazine 100 via the catheter. As the huge animal weaved alarmingly on his feet he then delivered a bolus of Ketamine, the knock down drug, via the same catheter.

Within eight to ten seconds the stallion sagged backwards on his rear end. Pete stepped out of the way of the collapsing horse and Jack pulled his head towards the ground on his right – leading him to fall into lateral recumbency – lying on his right side. For the first ten to fifteen seconds the muscles of the stallion's limbs twitched spasmodically. His eyelids flickered while his eyeballs rolled from side to side within their orbits. Slowly he succumbed in to relaxed anaesthesia. The twitching stopped, the eyes rolled gently back inside his head and his breathing became, relaxed, deep and slow, but regular.

Mick helped Joe tie a lead rope around the lower part of the topmost hind limb so that he could pull the leg backwards. Joe wrapped the rope around his back and leaned backwards gently pulling the leg out of the way. This gave Pete and Mick access to the damaged leg. Pete was already in position with his hands pushing into the blood soaked towels trying to minimise further bleeding.

Mick crouched over the damaged leg with surgical kits opened on the ground next to him. With a scalpel blade and scissors he quickly cut through the soaking red bandage. As he peeled the bandage open to expose the wound he was hit in the midriff and groin by a jet of blood fired from the horse's groin. Instinctively he pushed his fingers hard into the tissue above the wound and the blood slowed to a slight trickle immediately. He then pulled Pete's hand down and used it to replace his own – stemming the blood flow. A constant stream of blood still trickled from low in the wound and Mick used Pete's other hand to apply pressure to the leaking blood vessel below the wound.

Now the hard part started.

Mick delicately explored the wound – a twenty centimetre ragged tear in the skin extending at least fifteen centimetres deep into the muscles of the thigh. He extended the edges of the wound further up and down the thigh to get decent access to the deeper haemorrhaging tissues. He had to find the ends of the severed blood vessel. Initially he concentrated on the end nearest the stallion's body, furthest up the leg. Within a few minutes he had found and isolated a very large torn blood vessel. It was intimately associated with other vital structures which he suspected were a large nerve and a wildly pulsating artery. He did not want to compromise these in any way at all so decided against trying to dissect the end of the torn blood vessel free to allow easier access for ligation. He carefully applied a large artery forceps to the end of the damaged blood vessel. He then used a small round bodied needle to pass a length of thick PDS suture material around the blood vessel almost a centimetre above the artery forceps. Satisfied that the suture material was positioned well, he tied a ligature in place. He tightened the first throw, or layer, in the ligature as tight as he could without breaking the suture. The PDS cut into his fingers and he held tight until the pain in his fingers told him that he couldn't tighten the suture any further. Each new throw in the knot was held tight until his fingers ached. Usually he used five throws in a ligature knot for security. He used at least seven on the first ligature. He repeated the procedure with four more ligatures one above the other. Not that he was feeling paranoid at all. He just had to stop the bleeding. In any other situation two ligatures would have been plenty.

He then asked Pete to remove his fingers from their position in the tissue above the wound. Pete's callused fingers trembled as they slowly pulled away.

No fresh bleeding. The ligated blood vessel filled with blood above the ligatures but none escaped.

Mick then carefully removed the artery forceps from the torn end of the blood vessel while holding the very end of the tissue with some rat-toothed forceps.

No bleeding… maybe Pete's prayers were being answered. He replaced the ligated blood vessel back deep into the laceration where he had initially found it and once more watched closely for blood escaping. All good. There was no fresh blood flow from the ligated vessel. Mick realised that he was holding his breath, and had been for quite some time. He slowly let out his breath and still there was no leakage. He breathed slowly again but did not relax.

His patient was still breathing regularly and deeply. So far, so good. No need for more anaesthetic at this stage.

Mick carefully dissected down towards the other end of the torn blood vessel, deep into the bottom of the wound, but lower down the limb. Once he located the vessel he repeated the same procedure as he had on the upper end. Mick's focus was intense. The seconds seemed like hours. Each suture took an eternity. Only three ligatures this time. No fresh bleeding.

Mick gestured for Pete to remove his remaining hand from the tissue below the wound. He pulled his hand slowly away and both men stared into the hole in the stallion's leg. There was only a minor trickle of blood seeping up from the depths of the wound - very minor. Mick was happy that it was only oozing from the traumatised muscle and there was no further escape from either end of the severed blood vessel. Once again, so far, so good… They were not out of the woods yet.

Peter's hands were cramping badly and he could not move any of his fingers. He crawled away a few metres and retched into the sawdust.

Mick looked at him over the mass of the sleeping stallion.

"Pete you're an absolute champion mate! …A bit of a girl …but an absolute champion."

Over the next few minutes Mick cleaned the wound with a mixture of sterile saline and iodine scrub. He then debrided the wound –

removed dead or damaged tissue from within the wound. Next he closed the space over the blood vessels and nerves by pulling adjacent muscle tissue over the top of them using cat gut sutures. He then closed the skin deficit with a continuous cat gut subcutaneous suture and then multiple simple interrupted Armofil sutures in the skin itself. The stitch up was tedious. Mick was fastidious with his work and as the minutes passed his fingers became tired and worked slower and slower. Even threading the suture material onto the needle was hard work by the time he was suturing the skin. Eventually the last stitch was in place – the gaping hole had been closed. It had probably taken 30-40 minutes but the stallion had not needed any top up with more anaesthetic - probably because he was in such a weakened state before they had started.

The huge horse was still breathing and beginning to shiver. Mick's back was aching. He doubted if he'd ever stand straight again.

Joe released his rope from the uppermost back leg as Mick slowly stood up. He stretched painfully then grudgingly stooped again and dragged his surgical gear away from his patient.

It was amazing the horse was still in the land of the living. All four knew how close the animal had been to death and they all understood that he was not out of the woods yet, by a long way.

Over the next few minutes the stallion's shivering and muscle tremors became quite dramatic. Mick, Joe and Pete pushed him into sternal recumbency – lying upright on his chest – while Jake held his head. They laid thick horse blankets over his back.

Mick got Joe to warm up ten litres of Hartman's solution in a bucket of warm water. When the fluid was at body temperature it was then administered via a drip line into another cannula in the stallion's other jugular vein. The full ten litres was given intravenously over the next forty to forty-five minutes.

The stallion was also loaded up with Penicillin, 20cc by intramuscular injection, and Gentamycin, 10cc by intravenous injection to cover for infection. He was given 10cc of Flunixin Meglumine intravenously, an extremely potent anti-inflammatory, to reduce inflammation in the damaged tissues of the traumatised leg. He was also given Tetanus Toxoid and tetanus antitoxin. The last thing that was needed was for the horse to recover from this horrific trauma and then to die a few weeks down the track from tetanus. Mick then supplied Joe with bottles of Penicillin and Gentamycin for ongoing treatment over the next few days. He also dispensed a large tub of Phenyl Butazone to continue the anti-inflammatory treatment and give ongoing pain relief.

The four men were exhausted. They all stood and stared at the shivering mass of horse. They'd just witnessed a miracle. The horse should have been dead. For a long time no-one talked. They simply stood and watched as the stallion slowly became more aware of his surroundings. His ears started tracking sounds from the paddocks and the stables nearby. Eventually he started whinnying in response to calls from horses in the stables.

As the first light of the new day crept over the red rocky outcrops of the Burrawong Mountains, the stallion snorted three or four times and then clumsily rose to his feet. He shook dramatically and looked as if he would collapse again without taking a step. Pete and Jake both leaned into him to support him. After four or five minutes he took several tentative steps. He was vaguely ataxic but was bearing weight on his right hind leg. There appeared to be reasonable control... No nerve damage...

Mick examined him fully. His colour was still extremely pale. His heart rate was 90/minute. He was shivering grossly. His rectal temperature was 35.8... But he was still alive.

Mick gave instructions to all three men for ongoing nursing and thanked them all for their help. It had been a huge night and everybody had put in a huge shift. He looked at Pete and a broad grin spread across his face.

"If Joe ever sacks you Pete you can have a job with me. You were fantastic mate. There is one condition however - you're not allowed to vomit during surgery OK?"

All four men grinned at each other and shook hands.

As Mick painfully climbed into the Rodeo and waved to Jake and Pete. Joe grabbed and shook his hand firmly.

"Thank you so much Mick. That was just amazing. I was sure he was dead. We paid three and a half million dollars for him last week, and he's not insured yet…"

Mick sat silently taking in this new information. After the night he'd just had, nothing surprised him.

"…And Mick. I was truly sorry to hear about your father. He was a great man."

Chapter 4

Mick didn't drive nearly as fast on the return journey to Stewarts River Veterinary Hospital. He was absolutely exhausted. His body ached. He was slowly reliving and analysing every moment of the callout to the haemorrhaging stallion, a long time habit. Could he? Should he have done anything differently? He relived the placing of every suture, and the tying of every ligature, again and again in his head. But his mind wandered. Joe's parting words pulled his thoughts elsewhere.

"Truly sorry to hear about your father... He was a great man..."

Andrew Gallagher had been a great man. He'd been the doctor in Stewarts River for over 40 years. He'd delivered two generations of children. He'd saved countless lives. The town loved him. He had been a pillar of the community. He was a founding member of the Rotary Club and the tennis club. He had built a model medical practice in town which had grown to employ between four and five doctors at a time including Rashid Chowdry, a young Indian doctor who himself had now been in town for over 20 years – and was loved by all. Chowdry had married a local girl and had three beautiful daughters. He had been Mick's best friend for close to 20 years.

At the ripe old age of 68 Andrew had decided that Stewarts River could happily survive without him and had elected to take his skills abroad and help the poor and downtrodden of the world. He had signed up with Medecins sans Frontieres in 2011 and had spent the last few years working as a doctor in war stricken countries. He loved it and felt he had been preparing himself for this work all his life.

Four months ago he had been working at the Mrajeeb Al Fhood refugee camp in northern Jordan - a camp specifically built to house Syrian refugees fleeing the Syrian Civil war. The camp had been invaded by ISIS militia. Sixty refugees had been murdered. Two doctors, including Andrew Gallagher, and four nurses, all working for Medecins sans

Frontiers under the auspices of the World Health Organisation, had been ritually slaughtered. They were publically beheaded.

Mick and his family had been devastated. The whole Stewarts River community had been devastated. Such a tragic loss. Such a barbaric death. Such a waste of life…such a good life…

Mick had been tortured by nightmares ever since… Watching his father being beheaded again and again. The gruesome youtube video of James Foley, the American journalist killed by ISIS in 2014, replayed in his dreams with Andrew Gallagher in Foley's place. The nightmares were excruciating – vivid and graphic. Mick's torture endured unabated, despite alcohol and sleeping tablets.

Andrew's funeral had been a very public affair. Dignitaries came from all over Australia, including the Governor General and the deputy Prime Minister. The world's press had descended on the town: ABC, BBC, CNN, Al Jazeera, and many more. Mick and his family and friends had not been allowed to grieve privately. The phrase "Media Circus" did not even begin to explain the ridiculous way in which Mick's father's funeral became a vehicle for politicians to rant about American politics, ISIS and military funding, and for journalists to debate foreign policy and Syrian aid packages. The passing of Andrew Gallagher - one of the world's kindest and gentlest humanitarians, father, grandfather and friend - got lost along the way.

Nobody had paid attention to Rashid and Beatrice Chowdry physically holding Mick upright at his father's graveside as he cried like a child. No-one had mentioned the devastation of a grandchild and ex daughter-in-law, bewildered and broken by the unthinkable loss of someone so dear. No one mentioned the sentiment in the town that a genuine saint had been lost for every single person who lived there.

Mick had been interviewed on local TV – Network 1 WNSW - soon after the funeral. He was not in a good state of mind. When veteran reporter Lauren Gleeson had asked about ISIS activities, including the massacre at Mrajeeb Al Fhood, she had not expected the vehemence of Mick's reply. He had coldly stared into the camera lens and made a very blunt statement.

"The killing of innocent and unarmed women, children and old men is disgusting and cowardly..." As tears welled in his eyes and his voice quivered with raw emotion he added -" Come and try me you evil bastards – I'll give you something to think about – I won't be such a soft fucking target..."

The footage was cut and did not go to air on Network 1 WNSW that day as planned. Unfortunately some hot shot kid at the TV station thought the footage was wonderful and uploaded it to youtube. The video went viral - 35 million hits over 7 days. Mick unwittingly became an anti - ISIS hero the world over. He was an internet sensation. Once again the media went crazy with stories written in the world's tabloids in 23 languages. The video was then shown on every major TV channel on the planet. Mick received way more than his 15 minutes of fame. He was invited to talk on TV shows all over the world. Ellen Dejeneres' people had phoned and e-mailed multiple times. Reporters had camped in vehicles opposite the veterinary hospital for weeks on end. Since the interview for Network 1, Mick had declined to talk to any media at all.

What had followed had been multiple death threats from every pro ISIS nut case in Australia and many likeminded nut cases around the globe. Mick and his family had undergone multiple police and anti-terrorism briefings in the following weeks and months, and had initially been under strict surveillance by police and other government anti-terrorism bodies.

Realistically the general public lost interest within a couple of weeks of the TV interview, and as ISIS continued their atrocities in the northern hemisphere over the next four months , the police and the government anti-terrorism offices also lost interest in the Gallagher family in the sleepy outback town of Stewarts River.

Life was slowly heading back to normal, but Mick really missed his dad. They had been great mates. He still found it hard to believe such a vibrant and wonderful person had been taken from the world in such an abhorrent, barbaric way.

Life was slowly heading back to normal. Did Mick just think that? Normal? Well he was back to work and working hard. He had to pay the bills. His ex-wife now owned his house, his superannuation and his wine collection. He was living in the flat at the Vet Hospital. The settlement last year had been huge. He'd had to go into massive debt just to keep his veterinary practice working. If the truth were told he knew he still loved Fiona. She was the most wonderful thing that had ever happened to him. She was a nurse at the hospital - worked for his dad over 20 years ago. She was blonde, slim but curvaceous, beautiful clear blue eyes, vivacious and simply the nicest person in the whole world. Fuck he'd thrown it all away. If only he could keep his dick in his pants. And it wasn't as if she hadn't given him a second chance - on six or seven occasions. He had just pushed things way too far. Fucking hormones. Together they had a daughter Julia, the apple of Mick's eye. Just turned twenty-one years old, stunning like her mother, and studying Law at Sydney Uni. Julia had hated Mick's guts when he and Fiona had split up. Everyone knew that it was all Mick's fault. Julia's wrath had been unbearable. She had treated him like a leper. She refused to even acknowledge his existence for months on end. Slowly, they were beginning to build bridges. He knew she still loved him hugely. He knew that he'd hurt her as much as he'd hurt her mother. He knew he could not turn back the clock.

So life was slowly getting back to "normal", or as "normal" as it could be. Rosie at the diner told him that normal was just one of the settings on the washing machine. She was right about most things. He'd have to look closely at his washing machine and see if it had a setting for "Up to your eyeballs in shit."

Chapter 5

According to Rocking Roy on Country FM 102.2, "The station that plays the hits just for you", it had just gone 5:45 on a beautiful Sunday morning in God's own country in Western New South Wales. Rocking Roy was just about to get romantic and play some of his favourite love songs. As the intro to Pink's "Try" started, and her beautiful voice started ululating before singing words, Mick decided he was going to take a detour on the way back to Stewarts River Veterinary Hospital. He knew he shouldn't but he knew he was going to. He was going to detour through town and do a drive past of his old home, the home now owned by his gorgeous ex-wife.

He knew that he shouldn't take this particular detour but he was driven by poorly understood primitive, primordial, hormonal and psychotic forces. He just had to do it. The result of the excursion could be reassurance which he craved, or absolute torture which could be the end of him. He couldn't stop now that he'd decided.

His brain started debating with itself deep in his tired head. How on earth could he bonk like a rabbit all over town and still be possessive of his wife? His ex-wife in fact. Because she was looking after his child – Julia – and Julia should not be allowed to witness her mother doing anything at all with anyone else. How would that affect her? She was delicate. She had already been hurt by the divorce. Life had to be smooth for her while she studied. Mick knew that she was only home during uni holidays and on the occasional weekend during term times, but... He could have no imposters in the family home affecting her studies or interfering with her relationship with her mother or upsetting the applecart in any way at all... Oh God he loved Julia...He wanted to make sure life was the best for his beautiful Julia...

He shuddered as he remembered another early morning visit which had brought both him and Julia unstuck. It had happened a couple of years ago when he still lived at the home. It was a terrible day. He had walked in on Julia shagging Toby Bryant. Fuck it was terrible. The picture tormented him till this day. It was her nineteenth birthday and she was home from uni in Sydney for the holidays. He'd been out half the night doing a caesarean on a cow and had decided to deliver a huge bunch of flowers to Julia before he slid off to bed himself. He was rooted. It was about seven in the morning. He tapped on her door, heard a muffled groan and then entered the room – only to find Tim Bryant's lily-white arse going hell for leather between Julia's beautiful thighs. They were too engrossed in their exertions on top of the bed to notice him. He'd nearly dad a coronary.

Toby Bryant was her old boyfriend from school days. He worked for his father on a large cattle property seventy kilometres west of town. He was an exceptionally nice kid.

Mick thought that his head was going to explode. He was mortally offended. The indecency. Such an insult to him, her father, under his roof. She could not be doing this. She was naked and writhing like a snake. He couldn't unsee it. He went mental.

He smacked Toby over the head and pushed him off the bed. Julia screamed and pulled the bedclothes over herself. Tim didn't know what had hit him. Mick picked him up off the floor and threw him towards the bedroom door. Julia continued to scream. Fiona arrived in the doorway and instantly took in the situation. Two naked kids and a father, with a face the colour of beetroot, brandishing a mass of broken pink lilies. She positioned herself between Mick and Toby and told Mick quietly to calm down - they could sort this all out like adults. Mick had steam coming out his ears and Tim looked like a rabbit caught in the head-lights. Fiona bent and picked up discarded clothing from the floor and handed it to Tim. He had wanted the floor to open and swallow him whole, but now he grabbed his clothes and bolted. The front door crashed shut seconds later and Tim's ute blasted up the drive while the house was still shaking. Mick had often thought that poor Tim had probably driven all the way home stark naked. That was a hellish day. Happy nineteenth.

So why was he driving towards his old house now? Was he wanting to find Fiona entertaining a new bloke? At 6 o'clock in the morning any visitor would likely be on a sleep over. What on earth would he do if there was an extra vehicle parked in his drive? "His" drive? In his perceived territory? In his cave? He knew he was wanting reassurance. He wanted to make sure that Fiona had no overnight visitor. He just wanted to know. Amongst his gross failings he knew that he was possessive and extremely jealous where he had no right to be.

He couldn't stop himself.

Chapter 6

Mick drove through Stewarts River heading north. The town was still asleep. The main street was empty. There was no-one around at all. Even the coffee shops were still closed. No tables or chairs on the pavement. No umbrellas announcing Deano's Own Coffee Blend. They mustn't open till six, Mick thought. He passed the library and sat at a red light at the crossroads between Fotheringham Street and Stewart Street. As he waited on the light turning he looked down Fotheringham Street towards the river. The Jacaranda trees on the riverbank were in full bloom. They were quite stunning. He loved the majestic old trees with their masses of purple blooms. They were so beautiful.

The lights changed and he drove through the rest of the CBD with green lights all the way. The old town hall on his left looked like it was from a bygone era. It had imposing red sandstone walls, a grey slate roof, leadlight coloured windows and huge riveted wooden doors. It reminded him of old churches he'd visited in Europe. There were two banks, The National Australia Bank and the Commonwealth Bank, both announcing the lowest home loan rates in Australia... Both? The National Australia Bank owned Mick's vet practice, his debt and his soul. Regards his superannuation...that was a joke. It was long gone. His ex-wife could live off that for a long time. Grocery stores, electrical stores, butchers, bakers and candlestick makers made up the rest of the businesses which held the prime real estate on Stewart Street, the main drag through town. The street, like the town, was named after the grazier who first brought cattle to these parts, John Logan Stewart. Stewart was the son of convict stock. His father, Gregor Stewart, had been deported from Scotland for stealing sheep and his mother from Ireland for the same crime. Running stock must have been in their genes. Once freemen in Australia, the couple married and produced seven children. John Logan Stewart was the oldest. Some wonder if the cattle he brought to the valley were actually stolen, en route, from Sydney.

Mick passed the "Long Paddock Hotel" on his right. This was the number one pub in town. It was a beautiful building painted in Australian Heritage colours. The window frames and doors were painted purple and green, and the walls a pale buttermilk yellow. It's gorgeous old bull nosed verandas topped with corrugated iron roofing, were surrounded by ornate wrought iron railings and aged, gnarled grape vines climbed all over them. It was another stunning building, ancient by Australian standards – at least eighty years old.

Just past the pub sat "Stewarts River Memorial Park". The entrance to the park was through huge black iron gates with memorial walls on either side. The names of fallen diggers, the local men and women who had given their lives for their country during times of war, were inscribed in the walls on either side of the gates. A lone bronze soldier stood to attention on the wide pavement in front of the gates. The inscription written across the metal bars of the gates read "Lest We Forget".

Mick's mood grew sombre. He looked along the front of the park where new signage was being built in the busy flower beds. The "Stewarts River Memorial Park" was about to have a name change. Council had voted to re-name the park "Andrew Gallagher Park" in memory of Mick's father. The ceremony was to take place in two weeks, during the annual "Jacaranda Festival" celebrations. Mick was extremely touched. The park was one of his dad's favourite places on the planet. He had helped shape it over the years. He had planted many beautiful trees including the Jacarandas. He had helped landscape hedges and flowering shrubs around the kids play areas where there were sandpits, roundabouts and swings. Just five years ago he had helped design and build a skate park within the park for the teenagers who liked to think they were alternate by riding skateboards and wearing baggy trousers around their hips, revealing their undies and their bum cracks. His dad had played a big part in making the park a welcoming beautiful space, right in the town centre, where everyone in the community was welcome and all could come and enjoy.

Mick was really touched, but at the moment every time he saw the park his whole body filled with sadness. Sadness for a wonderful life that was cut way too short.

Mick drove passed the park picturing Andrew Gallagher in his head – laughing, drinking beer, and hugging his wife and his granddaughter under the beautiful Jacarandas. God he missed him.

Stewart Street continued north out of town, past the hospital, past the abattoir and on to the Luxcombe Highway. The highway led to Sydney 500km south-east and Brisbane 400km north-east. Mick turned off Stewart Street, to the right, just after the memorial park and onto Goldsmith's Bridge. The bridge was a 110 year old white painted metal bridge over the Stewarts River. As a kid Mick thought that it had been built out of meccano. Over the bridge the road joined the aptly named "Hanging Tree Road". This road led out of town to the cemetery and the ancient dead tree which stood on a small hill overlooking the cemetery like a crooked sentinel. Many horse thieves, cattle rustlers and bush rangers had allegedly been hanged from this tree in the early nineteen hundreds. Mick had often thought that it was quite efficient of the town council to hang people close to where they would be buried.

Once over the bridge Mick followed the road to the very edge of town where he turned right into Fallowfield Lane. When Mick had bought his property in Fallowfield Lane it had been a delightful, meandering dirt track opening up onto paddocks on either side with dense stands of old Ghost Gums every few hundred metres. The paddocks on the right had extended down to the river and looked over towards the town. The paddocks on the left had extended to the orange, brown haze of the horizon, with only the cemetery and "Hanging Tree Hill" breaking the flat monotony of the landscape about two kilometres from the lane. Back then, there had only been 7 or 8 houses, including his own, along the entire length of the lane. The lane was just under four kilometres long.

Since Mick had bought his property on Fallowfield Lane, all the neighbouring land had been sub-divided and then subdivided again. Today, there were entrances to properties every fifty or sixty metres on both sides of the road and it's tarred surface was easily wide enough for two vehicles to pass comfortably. The right side of the road was like "Wisteria Lane" in the "Desperate Housewives" TV series. Large city style bungalows sat on huge blocks with manicured gardens, where ride on lawnmowers were a necessity. The left side of the road, with the paddocks behind the house blocks, had been developed into dozens of small "farmlets". These had lovely big houses with room for stables and horse yards, or even small cattle yards, on the back part of the block. Most had access to the paddocks behind – ideal for horse owners and weekend farmers.

Mick had until recently owned number 316. The block was 3.16 kilometres from the junction at Hanging Tree Road. As he slowly approached his old home he could see the orange tiled house roof and the brown wooden stable block intermittently between neighbours houses and the large gum trees which still remained along the roadside.

He slowed to a crawl just as he reached the boundary of the property and crept along the road staring towards the house which was hidden by trees and garden shrubs. Two stunning Jacarandas stood in the middle of the front lawn. They were in full bloom and huge masses of coalescing purple flowers blocked Mick's view of the house. Low boughs hung just above the lawn and the upper branches climbed five or six metres into the sky. Every single millimetre had stunning purple flowers blooming. The grass was covered in a carpet of purple confetti. The morning sunlight had brought the trees alive with amazing, vivid colour.

Mick's focus had been stolen by the gorgeous flowering trees just as he reached the entrance to the drive. Suddenly his guts lurched. A large dirty, blue utility truck with a large silver work canopy was driving out of his garage and roaring up the drive towards the lane.

What the fuck? No.

No fucking way.

Half of his brain screamed at him to stop and block the driveway, but the other half forced him to speed up and drive past. He stared intensely into the cabin of the ute coming up the drive as he continued along the lane but could only make out dark sunglasses below a baseball cap.

Who the fuck?

As he continued slowly down the lane away from number 316 he stared wildly into his rear-view mirror.

The ute stopped momentarily at the top of the drive, then turned right towards Hanging Tree Road. As it turned, Mick's world moved in slow motion. The sign on the ute door was repeated on the side of the silver canopy. Mick saw it but refused to believe it.

"Bob Parsons and Sons – Stewarts River Plumbing"

Mick was hyperventilating. He was suddenly 15 out of 10 on the pissed off scale. His head was exploding. His guts were suddenly aching. No way. No fucking way. He screamed at the world.

"The dirty bastard! The dirty fucking bastard! Fuck...Fuck!"

Mick smashed his head on the steering wheel repeatedly. He felt nothing. Fiona was shagging Bob Parsons. Fucking hell. He was about ninety years old for fuck sake. Holy shit. Fuck.

Mick stopped his vehicle and pulled on the hand-brake. He switched the engine off. His hands were shaking. He was sweating.

He had to phone her. He had to tell Fiona she was making a huge mistake. Fuck. He knew that they'd played as a mixed tennis team a couple of times and had been at the same barbeques, but this was not, could not, be happening. Bob Parsons was a widower. He'd been on his own for over 10 years. He was as boring as bat shit. Fuck. He could not be shagging her.

He fumbled in his breast pocket for his phone. His fingers wouldn't work. He eventually pulled the phone out, but dropped it onto his lap. As he grabbed at it again it spun off his fingers, hit the dashboard and then fell down between his feet.

"For Fuck Sake..."

He knew that God was playing games with him.

He couldn't even see the phone, never-mind reach it.

A long tirade of expletives flew from his lips as he opened the Rodeo's door and climbed out onto the road. As he turned to search the floor of the vehicle the face of the phone lit up amongst the detritus in front of the driver's seat. The phone was ringing. The sound ominously filled the inside of the cab.

He stooped and picked the device up. He stared at the caller ID - "Fiona".

He stood and looked blindly into the blue morning sky. His brain screamed silently for several long seconds. Then he hit the receive button and lifted the phone to his ear.

Chapter 7

Mick held the phone to his ear and listened to a torrent of abuse from his ex-wife. She was screaming like a banshee. She was not happy.

"...You pathetic bastard...How low can you go? A drive by on a Sunday morning before sparrows fart... You're pathetic. How long are you going to stalk me for? We're not married any more Mick... I'm not a possession... When is this going to stop? You've absolutely lost the plot. Have you no dignity? Don't you care that you look like a complete dickhead behaving like this? I'm sick and tired of it Mick... You have completely lost the plot... Get Chowdrey to check your medication... You're an absolute loose bloody cannon... What on earth do you think you're doing?"

In a minor lull in the bombardment Mick ventured, "Why him? Why Bob Fucking Parsons? He could be your grandad..."

Fiona spat back, "He's fifty-eight Mick – only six years older than you... He's a gentleman Mick. He's honest and decent and he does NOT shag around..."

Mick could not respond to that without digging a bigger hole for himself. He decided to change tack.

"But if Julia finds out... It's a very delicate time in her life...Uni exams only two months away... It could upset the applecart badly... You know how upset she was when we split up."

"Grow up Mick. You never considered her when you were shagging your way around town. It didn't come into your thinking that behaving like a gigolo could affect your daughter. The whole school was talking about you shagging Linda fucking Cuthbert the week before her HSC exams. Don't you remember that? Maybe you don't remember her crying herself to sleep for weeks on end before her first term at uni because you had come home and meekly explained that you'd strayed with Lara fucking Docherty at the chemist. You only came clean because her hubby found you going at it doggy-style in the pharmacy and kicked the shit out of you. The kids in her netball team said you were maybe "picking up medication for a doggy" or "tending to a sick pussy". You don't remember her not eating, her visits to the doctor or her trips to counselling do you? Grow up Mick. She was probably relieved when we split up. Don't preach to me about upsetting the fucking apple cart. Don't be such a fucking arsehole. She knows about Bob already and she's delighted for me... Julia and Bob get along really well actually..." She waited for this to sink in.

Mick leaned on his Rodeo in stunned silence.

She twisted the knife.

"I think she likes the idea of a stable father figure..."

"Oh Fuck Off..." Mick exploded. "You're full of shit..."

"Why not ring and ask her? Or is she still not returning your calls?"

Fiona could be a grade A bitch when she felt like it and she was just winding up.

"What are you doing driving the streets at this time of day anyway? One of your tarts throw you out early?"

"Fuck off Fiona..." Mick was exasperated.

"No you fuck off Mick. It's time you grew up. Show your daughter that you can be a gentleman too. Stop giving her reasons to hate you. Stop stalking her mother."

"But Fi..."

"But nothing." She cut him off abruptly. "Now leave me alone before I call the police. I hear you're still best mates with all the boys at the station..." She was on fire and hitting way below the belt.

"Just fuck off Fi..."

"No Mick. You fuck off and get a real life. Stop fucking up mine and Julia's."

Mick could not respond. He felt like shit. He felt betrayed. He felt small. He felt inept. He felt mad as hell. There were tears in the corners of his eyes.

Fiona continued, "And if I hear that you've gone anywhere near Bob I will come after you and remove your testicles with your father's pruning shears. Are you with me?"

Mick could not reply. Fiona could hear his heavy breathing on the other end of the line. Her final assault was inspiring, worth ten out of ten for vitriol and timing.

"Do you know a question that I've asked myself repeatedly over the last few years?"

She paused. There was no response.

"How could such a great man as Andrew Gallagher produce an arsehole of a son like you?"

She knew it was cruel. She knew it would hammer him hard. She knew that he had worshipped his father. But by God he had pissed her off something shocking this morning. Mick Gallagher had pissed off the whole world over and over again during the last few years. He deserved it.

Mick stood frozen and numb on the end of the phone. The line went dead. She'd hung up.

It all hurt. Every word she'd said had rung true. He had been an awful husband. He had been an awful father. He had often wondered what his own father had really thought about his ridiculous lying and womanising. He was sure he had also been a very disappointing son.

Mick stood on the road and stared at the wind. He was tired. He was humiliated. He was very, very sad.

He turned to look back up Fallowfield Lane when he heard a vehicle on the road behind him. It was Fiona's white Toyota Hilux pulling out of the drive at 316 and turning towards town. As he watched the vehicle pull away down the road Fiona's arm extended out the driver's window and she delivered him the bird – her middle finger raised to the sky.

He didn't know whether to laugh or cry.

God knew he still loved her more than anything else on the planet.

Chapter 8

Mick slowly trundled back through town. There was still very little traffic. Deano's umbrellas were out over the tables on the pavement and early patrons were seated drinking steaming hot coffee and reading Sunday papers. Mick scarcely noticed them. He was on auto-pilot.

His conversation with Fiona played over and over in his head. Every single part of the conversation had hurt, but now every insult was sinking in. His conscious brain was taking him to a very unhappy place. His subconscious brain was on overdrive looking for meaning in what was not said and putting bizarre and ridiculous emphasis on every single syllable of every single word that she had uttered.

"Get Chowdry to check your medication," she had screamed. Did everyone know that he was on anti-depressants after the separation? Had she broadcast that to the whole world? Did the whole world think he was a fruit loop? Fuck. He knew he didn't need the fucking drugs anyway. He only took them to keep Chowdry happy. Two hundred milligrams of Zoloft a day was nothing. Half the world was on Zoloft. He didn't need it. How the fuck did she know? He was fucking pissed off now. That meant they were no fucking use. An absolute waste of time. She was just a fucking bitch. A real fucking bitch. His brain needed a swear jar.

Julia was returning his calls these days. Things were getting a lot better. Or was that just because she needed him to fix her horse?

Linda fucking Cuthbert. She was a music teacher at Stewarts River High, twenty-six or twenty-seven years old and just out of uni. Mick had met her first at a Parent-Teacher night, then again a couple of weeks later over a guinea pig with overgrown incisors. It was his last consult of a long day. She told him she'd shout him a beer at the pub. He couldn't refuse. Skinny with no tits, but her fiancé was miles away, teaching in Victoria. Only bonked her quietly for a few weeks and serviced the guinea pig as needed. The bitch gave him the clap. Chowdry had been very impressed with that – gave him a real bloody lecture. "Keep your dick in your pants for Chrissake. You have a beautiful wife and daughter and you could jeopardise your whole relationship…" The lecture had gone on for over an hour. His best mate made him feel like absolute shit. Fuck.

He didn't want to think about Lara fucking Docherty. She was separated from her husband now, but still worked at the pharmacy. She held Mick responsible for her predicament. She was renting a small house on the edge of town and had custody of her two teenage daughters. She had expected Mick to look after her. Fat chance – he wasn't the first and he was sure he wouldn't be the last. She was the reason he had to drive to Albeston every couple of months to get his Zoloft script filled. A round trip of over two hundred kilometres. Bitch.

A niggling pain was starting to throb inside his head. He was fading. He was knackered. He needed food and caffeine. He was heading for "Smitho's Servo" on the south side of town. It was on his route back to the vet hospital. He'd fill up on fuel there and grab some coffee. If Rosie was cooking in the diner he'd treat himself to a big cooked breakfast. Suddenly he could smell cooked bacon and was salivating like Pavlov's dogs.

Rosie Smith was "Smitho's" wife and Mick Had known them both since school days. "Smitho" had run the service station on the Main Road out of town since his dad had died back in the mid-eighties. There was only one son to continue the family business and he took over the reins easily and soon turned into his dad. He was more like his dad than his dad was in both looks and personality.

So why had Mick not turned into his own father?

Smitho had been married to Rosie for over thirty years. They'd been high school sweethearts. Lucky bastards. Thirty years. But then, as Mick looked at it, Smitho had never sampled forbidden fruit - often the most delicious - or if he had, he had never been caught.

Mick loved them both, and their three kids, and their three cats, and their dog. The whole family including the animals suffered from the excesses of Rosie's kitchen. Smitho had always been as skinny as a matchstick but now, at the ripe old age of fifty-two, he was developing a small paunch for the first time in his life. The kids were plain fat, and the cats and the dog were grossly obese. Rocky, a thirty-two kg Staffordshire Bull Terrier, was currently on a drip in the vet hospital suffering from acute pancreatitis – no doubt as a result of a meal of left over lipids from Rosie's kitchen. Rocky was like two dogs stuck together with only one head and four legs. He looked like a small hairy snooker table. He was the happiest and friendliest dog on the planet.

Rosie herself was huge. She was not tall. She was however very wide and very round. Her arse stuck out behind her as if she had a small mattress stitched to her buttocks. Her midriff was simply enormous. Mick imagined she had not seen her feet for a long time – unless she had looked in the mirror. Her boobs were like huge watermelons. Her cleavage was one of the wonders of the natural world. Probably the hottest deepest, most mysterious ravine in the universe. Mick had often wondered how skinny little Smitho had never been sucked in there and lost forever. Maybe the new paunch was insurance. Rosie had the loveliest smooth, pink skin, dark brown eyes and forever laughing full lips. Her hair changed colour with the wind. It could be red, blonde or even purple on consecutive days. She loved smut and dirty jokes. Sexual innuendo was a lifelong habit. Rosie was always vibrant and happy. Rosie could always cheer Mick up. Mick sure needed cheering up today.

He pulled in beside the diesel bowser and started to fill up the huge diesel tank. He had a secondary tank in case of emergencies, but preferred not to use it if possible. He always topped the main tank up when he could. As the bowser gurgled and whirred, Smitho appeared on his shoulder carrying a windscreen washer. Smitho looked unshaven and unkempt. His balding head shone above a tangled mass of long, wispy grey hair which grew from just above ear level. His ragged overalls were covered in years' worth of oil stains. It was good to know that some things never changed.

Smitho grinned from ear to ear revealing a large gap where his two upper middle incisors should have been. His eyes twinkled.

"Morning Mickus…Been out delivering babies or just practicing making them?" He sniggered at his own humour.

A smile grudgingly stole onto Mick's face. He returned fire.

"Is your missus cooking this morning or is she too tired from last night's sexploits to get out of bed?"

As Smitho wiped the grime off all the windows on the filthy truck he replied, "She was out jogging at five o'clock this morning then snuck home for a quickie before work. You should know – an active sex life keeps you in tip-top form. She's in there slaving over a hot griddle even as we speak. She just loves the idea of tending to a hot sausage whenever the need arises."

"I hope she washed her hands before she started mixing the burger mince."

Smitho stopped in mid window-wipe. Suddenly he looked very serious. After several moments thought he stated, "Oh no. She never does that."

Both men giggled like kids. Mick felt vaguely relaxed for the first time that day. He continued, "I'm heading in for brekky. You got time for a coffee?"

"Love to," Smitho announced. "Just got to phone Telecom first. The bloody EFTPOS is out again this morning. I'll join you shortly."

He patted Mick on the back and turned and ambled off towards the service station office. Mick could hear Smitho chortling to himself as he went. "Never thought about that. Maybe we should charge extra for the beef burgers..."

The diesel bowser eventually grumbled to a halt and Mick absently looked at the gauges and meters attached to the long black hose he was holding.

"Fucking Hell!" Mick had just put $107.14 worth into his tank. Ah well. Nothing he could do about it. He needed it. Note to self however – better put the travelling charges up.

He jumped back inside the Rodeo and drove out of the petrol station forecourt and onto the parking area out the front of the restaurant. The restaurant and the service station were both under the same roof and occupied roughly half of the long flat building each. The service station had three covered work bays and a large storage area for parts, and a small office opposite 6 fuel bowsers. Smitho's tow truck and the vehicles he towed back for repair were all stored round the back of the building. The restaurant – "Rosie's Diner" – was large and comfortable and could seat well over a hundred patrons. It was the busiest spot in town on cattle markets days and "killing days" at the abattoir.

The doorbell buzzed as he entered the restaurant and a high pitched voice shouted from the direction of the kitchen.

"Milk and two Mickus?"

"That would be lovely thanks Rosie," Mick called back and then slowly plodded down to the long breakfast bar overlooking the kitchen where Rosie and two other female staff were hustling and bustling over hissing cook tops. He climbed onto a stool, folded his arms on top of the benchtop in front of him and laid his head on his arms as if to go to sleep. The steady clunking of cutlery, the heat from the cooktops and the piped music from "Country FM 102.2" was all very comforting. If he had a pillow he could have drifted off to sleep quite happily. He could hear Ivor Davis of Icehouse singing "Great Southern Land..." God, the eighties. Great times.

His reverie was interrupted as Rosie planted a big wet kiss in his ear and clunked a steaming mug of coffee on the bench in front of him. He sat up to see the beautiful Rosie hanging over the bench in front of him. Her hair was Barbie pink, along with her eyeshadow and her lip gloss. She had squashed her boobs down on top of the bench making her cleavage deeper than the Marianna Trench. She was grinning happily. Her eyes twinkled like diamonds.

"I know you're hot for me Mick," she gasped. She gave her cleavage a little more air by pulling down the low neckline of her uniform. Her boobs were monstrous...of truly biblical dimensions. "Why don't we just make it official Mick? Why don't we just have sex here on the counter, tell Smitho he's had it too good for too long and then elope to the Gold Coast?"

Mick stared into her beautiful brown eyes.

"Sorry Rosie. I've got to wash my socks today."

Rosie twinkled some more. "How are you Mickus? You look rooted. Long night?"

Mick sighed. "Yeah. Huge Rosie. I think the call came in about two am. Big stitch-up out at Athena Stud. Stallion staked himself in the groin. Bleeding everywhere. Very messy. Long, long job. Haven't made it back to bed yet." He yawned widely as if just realising how little sleep he'd actually had.

"So what d'you want to eat honeybunch? We need to get you fed and then get you straight home to bed. We can do you anything at all. But after the sock washing comments – I'm off the menu." She squinted her eyes and pretended to scowl.

"I'm absolutely starving Rosie. Could I have one of your world famous fry-ups with hash browns and extra mushrooms please?"

"For you my angel - anything at all."

Rosie screamed the order loudly over her shoulder and both the other girls shouted back from the bowels of the kitchen, "Yes Chef."

Rosie grinned. "We've been watching Masterchef."

Mick laughed and took a long pull on his coffee. It was hot, sweet, bitter and delicious.

"That's great coffee Rosie"

"You like that Honey? Deano at the coffee shop makes that up for us special. He's a good kid. Smitho thinks he's trying to get into my pants."

As Mick tried not to laugh again he sprayed a fine mist of coffee all over the bench. He couldn't make up his mind whether to laugh or choke.

"I thought you said you liked it." Rosie glowered at him again as she reached for a kitchen cloth to wipe away the lost coffee.

Mick drank more as Rosie positioned herself directly in front of him across the bench. She looked at him for some long seconds. He steadily returned her gaze. Eventually Rosie spoke.

"So what's the matter Mick? You look like shit. You really do. Somethings not right. What's going on?"

Mick continued to stare at Rosie. He knew this was why he'd come here. He wanted to talk to someone. Shit - he wanted to scream at someone.

The buzzer at the door announced the arrival of another patron. Mick heard footsteps moving steadily up behind him. The stool next to him was dragged a few inches across the floor and then Smitho was sitting next to him at the breakfast bar. Mick turned and smiled inanely at him. Smitho had read his wife's body language and knew this was no time for witty banter. He looked poker faced at Mick and asked diplomatically, "So what the fuck's up Mick?"

Mick looked from Smitho to Rosie and back again.

Silence.

He dropped his eyes to stare at his coffee cup. No one spoke. Eventually Mick eventually forced the words out but he couldn't look at either of them.

"Fiona's shagging Bob fucking Parsons."

The quiet words sat in the air for everyone to digest.

After a few seconds Smitho leaned over and put his arm around his friends' shoulders. Rosie reached across the bench squeezed his hand. There were no words.

One of the kitchen staff arrived and placed a steaming hot plate of food in front of Mick. When she realised the gravity of the moment she evaporated into thin air.

"Bob fucking Parsons." Mick repeated, still staring vacantly into his coffee.

Rosie squeezed his hand tighter and started the painful conversation.

"It was always going to happen sooner or later Mick. She's a very attractive woman. You've been parted almost two years. You can't expect her to be on her own for ever."

Mick interrupted, "But Julia stays there when she's back from uni. She can't bloody entertain in front of Julia..."

The silence before Rosie's next words was deafening.

"Julia's a big girl now Mick. You can't keep her wrapped up in cotton-wool for ever. And Bob Parsons is a really nice guy. He's got a lovely manner. His kids are gorgeous and he pretty well brought them up on his own after his wife got sick. She could have picked up any of a hundred other dead shits from around here. I think you're lucky she picked a good one..."

Mick was wading in treacle. He wanted his buddies to rant about Fiona's behaviour – tell him she was no good - tell him she was an absolute selfish bitch - tell him she had lost the plot. He wanted them to tear strips off Bob Parsons – to tell him that he was a scumbag - tell him that he should have been put down at birth - tell him that the arsehole should never be allowed anywhere near his family... Instead they were fucking well reassuring him that this was a good situation... Bullshit! This was absolute fucking bullshit!

His voice was cracking as he almost shouted to emphasise his dismay, "She's shagging Bob Parsons - Bob fucking Parsons."

Smitho squeezed his shoulder one more time. The stool scraped the floor beside him and he listened to footsteps moving across the tiles towards the door. The door-bell buzzed as the door opened quietly and then slowly shut.

Mick looked at Rosie. She stared across the breakfast bar and regarded him sadly.

"How long Rosie?"

"Maybe two or three months Mick."

"...And I'm the last to know?"

"You usually are Mick. You spend too much time with your head up your own arse to see what's going on around you."

Somebody else was hitting below the belt now. Frustratingly he knew it was all true. Too frigging true. He just didn't need to be told. He sat and stared at Rosie. He was cold and numb. His brain had stopped working. He wondered why he'd ever come here. He thought these guys were his friends. What the fuck was going on. Everybody hated his guts. Everybody was treating him like his wife shagging somebody else was no big fucking deal. He needed reassurance that it was all wrong and could not be happening. All fucking wrong. Smitho hadn't said a single word. Fuck.

Rosie pushed his breakfast plate closer to him.

"Come on Mick. Better eat your brekky before it's stone cold."

Mick wasn't hungry anymore.

"Sorry Rosie. I've lost my appetite."

She reached across the bench and took hold of his hand again. She held it tight and looked straight into his eyes.

"Look honey, I know it hurts, but give it time. Bob is a good bloke. If it works out I'm sure he'll treat her really well. And Julie. She's becoming her own woman now. She'll make up her own mind. She's tough. She's resilient."

She continued to look into his tired eyes. After a few moments she gently whispered, "The woman is a saint. How she put up with you for so long I still have no idea. Be nice to her Mick. She's the mother of your daughter. She's still a very important part of your life."

Mick croaked quietly, "You're right. I've been no angel."

Rosie didn't bat an eyelid.

"No Mick you've been an absolute fucking arsehole. But me and Smitho still love you. Weird eh?"

She paused but her gaze stayed fixed deep in Mick's eyes.

"And your latest romance is causing more ructions on the Stewarts River grapevine than Fiona's is... You really are a fucking dickhead." She sounded exasperated. She shook her head slowly from side to side but her gaze did not falter.

Mick did not want to acknowledge what she'd just said. Suddenly he was more pissed off than he could remember ever being. How the fuck did Rosie know? He thought nobody knew. He thought he'd quietly scored himself a goddess. Who the hell else knew? This was just too much.

Rosie broke Mick's train of thought. She was tugging the neckline of her top south again. Her colossal boobs were coming up for air. Her eyes were twinkling like diamonds.

"So do you want a quick shag on the counter before the paying customers arrive or what?"

He leaned across the counter and planted a delicate kiss on her shiny pink lips.

"Sorry dear, maybe next time. I really do have a lot of socks to wash."

The banter came automatically. His brain was in turmoil. Today had all been too much... And it wasn't even seven o'clock yet. He stood slowly and turned away from the counter. It felt like it took the best part of an hour to reach the door. As he pulled it open he called over his shoulder.

"Can you feed my breakfast to Smitho? He looks like he's fading away to a shadow. He tells me he's being worked too hard."

Rosie's shrill voice shrieked back, "Can you take it and give it to my poor dog? I hear that you're starving him to death at your vet hospital..."

Mick turned in the doorway and looked back at his second best friend in the world.

"That dog could live off his back for a year or more without food. I'll give you a ring about him later in the day."

He blew Rosie a kiss and headed out into the warm September sun.

As he drove away from town, towards the Rankin Bridge, he rehashed the latter part of the morning in his head. Rosie was right. She always was. He should let Fiona go. He had messed up her life too much already. He knew it was the right thing to do. The only thing to do. He just couldn't. As for Julia - she definitely was growing into her own woman. But she was her mother's daughter.

Thinking of Julia brought his thoughts back to the day ahead. He had her 12 year old gelding Zeus, on a drip in the stables at the vet hospital. He had anaesthetised him the day before to remove a fractured splint bone from his near-side front leg. Yep, Mick realised it was time to start thinking about work again. Zeus would need anti-inflammatories, antibiotics and a dressing change this morning. Only a couple of kilometres and he'd start all over again.

Chapter 9

The battered Rodeo crunched to a halt in the gravel yard behind Stewarts River Veterinary Hospital. The Veterinary Hospital had been built four years previously. It was 4km from the outskirts of town. There was plenty of room there with paddocks and stables for horses and a set of reasonable cattle yards with a good cattle-crush so that farmers could bring cases to Mick instead of paying him to travel out to them. Some of the outlying properties serviced by the practice were over two hundred kilometres away. Farmers bringing cases to Mick saved themselves hundreds of dollars in travelling fees and saved Mick hours of unproductive time sitting in his truck. The main Hospital building itself was an old wooden farmhouse with a huge Queensland style veranda all round. The farmhouse had lent itself very well to conversion to a Veterinary Hospital. The building sat on the western side of the main road south out of town. It consisted of a large waiting room, two consult rooms for small animal consultations, an office, a large drug dispensary, a prep room where animals were knocked out and prepared for surgery, a large theatre for surgery and a large hospital ward which could hold upwards of 20 small animals at a time.

Out the back the large gravel yard had a row of four wooden stables on the south side and the cattle yards and the crush a short distance away on the north side. There was good truck access and a sturdy loading ramp which facilitated the easy loading and unloading of cattle. Between the yard and the paddocks beyond, were a large shed which was used to store the practice vehicles and farm equipment, and a small granny flat built just off the shed. The flat had been built as a residence for locums and vet students but now Mick called it "Home Sweet Home". It consisted of a large sitting room with a rudimentary kitchen and a small bedroom which almost fitted a double bed inside. A small toilet and shower room were accessed from the bedroom. It was definitely not a luxury bachelor pad.

As Mick stepped out of the truck he sensed something was amiss. The door of the stable, where he had left Zeus on his intravenous fluids the evening before, was slightly ajar. Shit. Mick hoped he'd decided to stay put and not gone for a wander.

Mick crossed the yard, pulled the stable door wide open, and stepped into the shaded interior. Immediately the hairs stood up on the back of his neck and a cold numbness enveloped his body. He knew someone had just walked over his grave.

Soft yellow light from the skylight illuminated a bizarre and surreal scene. It took several seconds to make sense of what he was seeing in front of him. Suddenly he was wide awake. The stable was an absolute blood bath. The straw beneath his feet was blood soaked and matted with huge gelatinous, red blood clots. Congealed purple blood sat in pools on the bare concrete where the straw had been violently thrashed away. Red foam and froth straddled the straw from one blood pool to the next. There was blood sprayed across every wall as if someone had stood in the middle of the stable with a red fire hose and haphazardly blasted in all directions. Blood clots hung from the ceiling like stringy red/purple stalactites and small tacky red drips dropped in slow motion to the floor. On the far side of the stable lay Zeus. He looked grotesque. He was wedged upside down against the wall with his two right legs rigidly extended upwards. His left hind limb was rigidly folded against his abdomen. The left forelimb was lost under blood covered bedding. He was still and stiff and blood covered. There was complete silence, punctuated only by an occasional soft plop as a blood drop landed in a blood pool on the floor. Mick had stopped breathing. His brain was trying to make sense of this. This could not be real. This was fucking ridiculous. Just fucking unreal. As he stepped closer to the lifeless form of the horse a hellish realisation chilled his very soul. The horse had no head. A mangled stump of muscle, vertebrae, spinal cord and shredded trachea protruded from the torso. Stringy red black blood clot clung to every exposed tissue.

The stable was spinning. Mick slumped against the wall. He suddenly had severe gut cramps. He fell to the floor and vomited. He vomited up yellow fluid, again and again. The pain from the vomiting was excruciating. He hadn't eaten in hours. When there was nothing left inside he continued to retch. The pain was severe. His guts ached and his chest burned. The vomitus stuck in his nose and throat made him choke. He coughed and wheezed and retched. His eyes burned as they filled with acid tears and his vision blurred till all he could see was a blurred red haze.

Eventually he slowed his breathing and composed himself. He made himself reassess the situation. He had to look again. He had to confirm that this nightmare was actually real. He wiped his eyes painfully on the rough material of his overalls and stole another look at his daughter's beloved horse. It was an absolute mess. Dead. Beheaded.

No head. What the fuck? Dead. No fucking head. This could not be real.

No head.

Just like his father.

Jesus Christ - ISIS. It couldn't be. It could just NOT be. But who the hell else could have done this?

Fucking hell.

Mick had to get out of the stable - get some fresh air. He had to get his brain working again. He slowly climbed to his feet and stumbled through the stable door into the warm early morning sunlight. He leaned his back against the stable wall and tried to compose himself. He inhaled slowly and deeply. He stood there for several minutes waiting for his head to clear. He could make no sense of the situation.

This could not be happening. As he tried to focus on the yard in front of him the top of the stable door exploded right next to him. A split second later he saw a flash of light out of the corner of his eye and the right side of his chest seemed to explode also. The pain was excruciating. Suddenly he had no breath in his lungs. His head smacked back onto the wall behind him and his legs buckled. As he hit the ground large splinters of wood ricocheted around the yard as the wall of the stable was blown apart behind him. Fresh blood was seeping through his torn overalls, where the pain was intense, high on the side of his chest. What the fuck??? His brain was screaming in disbelief. This could not be real. Sudden realisation cleared his shocked head. He had to move. He was being shot at by some bastard with a high powered rifle from beyond the cattle yards. He had to move or he was dead. No way. No fucking way.

Mick lurched to his feet and tried to bolt across the yard. His legs were leaden. Every stride took a mammoth effort of will. The pain in his chest blasted to ridiculous new levels. As he clumsily weaved towards the vet hospital, more shots obliterated the walls of the stables and ripped through the gravel behind him. It took an eternity to cover six or seven metres. He thought each step might be his last. But he could not die here. Not like this. Not now. He threw himself onto the veranda where he rolled and landed in a heap against the back door of the hospital. His chest screamed with the most hellish pain and he could not get breath into his lungs but he knew he had to get inside at any cost. He was dead unless he got inside. From the floor of the veranda he kicked the door savagely till it flew open. He screamed with agony as he rolled onto his stomach and then desperately crawled inside. Once through the door he could go no further. The pain in his chest was off the Richter Scale. His right arm would not work without sending electric shocks through the rest of his body. Even the slightest movement of his arm sent searing pain to the backs of his eyes making his vision ebb and flow. He had to stop here. Just for a moment. Just till the pain went. Just till he could breathe again.

He lay on the floor and concentrated on breathing. Each breath was excruciating, but he had to breathe. He had to overcome the pain. He had never encountered pain like this before. It was truly hellish - intense and debilitating. Any movement at all made the pain reach new and impossible heights. Why was this happening? What on earth was going on? He could not comprehend what had just happened. What was happening now? This could not be real. This had to be a dream. The pain was beyond belief. How on earth could this be?

He found himself praying - praying for the pain to go. Where the words came from he did not understand. This was his first prayer since childhood.

Chapter 10

There had been no shots for several minutes. Mick still lay on the floor concentrating on breathing. He had found that if he breathed short and shallow breaths the pain was markedly reduced. He had also realised that his right arm still functioned OK and he could move it fairly well – but when he attempted to move his shoulder then severe pain shot through his chest and his head. As his chest wall moved, with every short breath, he could feel the grating of broken ribs. For several minutes he focused purely on his breathing. Then slowly he realised that after the explosive noise of the initial attack all had gone extremely quiet.

The silence was deafening. Had the shooter moved? Was he waiting for Mick to show himself again? Was he coming to the building? Mick had to move. He had to phone for help. He cursed quietly. He had left his mobile in the Rodeo. There was no heading back out there. He'd be a dead man in an instant. He had to get to the office.

Slowly and painfully Mick rose. The pain in his chest was constant with excruciating sharp lightning bolts to his head very time he moved his right shoulder. The corridor spun and iridescent white spots floated in front of his eyes. As he took his first step the small window above him shattered and a large hole was ripped in the opposite wall just in front of his head. He crashed back onto the floor. His chest, shoulder and head screamed with a new explosion of debilitating pain. The pain was beyond comprehension. He fought to stay conscious. He fought to breathe. As he lay on the floor the wall above him exploded into splinters of wood and plaster board as more shots erupted from outside.

Beyond the pain his brain still functioned. Primordial instincts. He had to move. He had to stay alive. He crawled along the floor through the dust and flying debris towards the office. Every movement was hideously painful. The minutes it took him to claw his way to the office door felt like a lifetime. Inch by inch, floorboard by floorboard. He concentrated through the pain. His focus was purely to get into the office. It should be a safe haven. It was in the centre of the building and there were no windows. He would be safe there. As he eventually crawled through the office door he was vaguely aware that the shooting had stopped again but a constant ringing in his ears made it difficult to hear anything at all.

Mick lay still on the office floor. With no new physical exertion the excruciating pain subsided dramatically. As the pain decreased he was able to concentrate and focus on a game plan. He had to contact the outside world. He desperately needed help. He had to get to the office phone.

The phone was on the desk in the middle of the office. He carefully climbed to his feet and stood for several long moments as the room spun around him and then settled down. He walked slowly and painfully to the desk and then carefully slumped into his office chair. The firm contours of the padded chair supported his aching back and ribs and for a few seconds he breathed longer deeper breaths. As he reached for the phone he realised that something was not right. There were no lights or messages lit up on the console of the phone. He put the phone to his ear with his left hand and then had to stifle a scream as he reached to hit the switch for an outside line with his right. Pain blasted from his shoulder deep into his head. FUCK!!! Do NOT move your shoulder you dickhead... He slowly crept the fingers of his right hand across the desk and managed to hit the button. There was no tone at all. The phone was dead. Shit. Fucking shit. The bastard outside had prepared for any scenario.

Mick opened the top drawer of his desk and pulled out a handful of keys. He pocketed the keys for the spare utility truck that he kept in the back shed and picked out a small unlabelled key. He slowly bent beneath the desk and inserted the small key in the door of the safe hidden there, fixed to the floor. Bending under the desk made his head spin and indistinct white shapes once again clouded his vision. He concentrated hard and pulled the safe door open. He then lifted out a small grubby cloth bag and spilled it's contents on top of the table. There were several bottles of Morphine and Ketamine, and several packets of Temgesic vials and Temgesic tablets. He selected a bottle of morphine and a couple of packets of Temgesic vials and pushed them into the breast pockets of his overalls.

He then rose and slowly walked to the open door on the other side of the office. This door led into the prep room where on normal days animals were prepared for surgery – anaesthetised, intubated and surgery sites shaved, before being taken into the operating theatre next door. The room was lined with shelves containing boxes of syringes, needles, catheters, fluid bags, giving sets, electric clippers, bandages and dressings etc., etc., from floor to ceiling. There were two tables in the centre of the room – one a normal examination table and the other a "wet-prep" table with a stainless steel gridded cover over a large sloping sink. Like the office there were no windows in the prep room. Mick made his way to the table with the sink and emptied his breast pockets onto the stainless steel grid. He stared at the Morphine and the Temgesic. He knew that the morphine would give him almost immediate pain relief but it would also affect his brain and his judgement. He did not need that. He had to stay as sharp as possible. This particular drug could also cause respiratory depression and he was having enough problems breathing as it was. Temgesic it was then.

He selected a 5ml syringe and a 12 gauge short needle from the boxes on the shelves. He opened the packet of Temgesic ampoules and awkwardly flicked the tops of all five of the 1 ml ampoules in the first pack. He opened the syringe wrapping and firmly placed the needle onto the end of the syringe. The pain in his right shoulder was moving up a few gears. He was having to use both hands and concentrate on the coordinating fine hand movements to load the drug into the syringe. His fingers were shaking. Inserting the needle into the open hole in the cracked ampoules was frustratingly slow and the recurring floating white shapes in front of his eyes only slowed the process further, but eventually he had 5mls of Temgesic loaded up in the syringe. He had no idea of the dose for humans. He knew an adult German Shepherd could be given 2-3 mls. He was a fair bit bigger than a German Shepherd.

His plan was to remove his overalls and give the injection intramuscularly. When he tried to open the studs of his overalls on the front of his chest however the crescendo of pain made his knees buckle.

Once again his mouth filled with the acid taste of vomitus. He clung agonisingly to the side of the prep table and stayed unmoving until the nausea subsided.

With his left hand he picked up the drug loaded syringe and suddenly plunged the needle into the muscle of his left thigh - straight through his overalls. In the same movement he hammered the plunger of the syringe and pushed 5mls of Temgesic directly into his left quadriceps muscle. Surprisingly there was no pain felt in his leg but the sudden lightning bolt to his head and his eyes made him collapse onto the tiled floor. His chest and shoulder pain blasted to new heights. The pain in his head was excruciating and he could see nothing at all apart from blinding, white, pulsing lights.

Chapter 11

Mick had no idea how long he'd spent on the floor. He had no idea whether or not he'd lost consciousness. He was aware that there had been more rifle shots into the building.... But now the shots were coming from the south side of the hospital and he could hear windows and walls smashing in the kennel room next door. He could also hear dogs barking and whining. The shelves in the prep room shuddered with every new explosion of noise from next door.

Mick was aware that his breathing was less laboured than previously and the pain in his head and chest were now just dull aches. Moving his right shoulder was still painful but it was way more manageable than earlier. Using the metal leg of the prep sink as a support he climbed slowly to his feet.

No more shooting. The shooter had been on the north side of the building earlier. Had he changed position or was there more than one shooter? He stood and listened for several minutes. No noise at all.

He gently pulled apart the studs on the front of his bloodied overalls all the way down to his waist. With his left hand he shoved the shoulders of the overalls down his arms and slowly wriggled his arms out of the sleeves. The overalls sagged to his waist and he could now see the wound on his chest. He had a 12 centimetre by 8 centimetre ragged skin deficit high on the right side of his chest just below his armpit. Beyond the skin edges were a purple bloodied mush of dried blood and torn muscle. Dried blood covered his whole right side down into his underpants. There were stringy bits of yellow froth and dried blood matted in the hair of his armpit. He could see vaguely white solid looking structures deep amongst the muscle debris in several spots. Probably ribs. Probably broken. He could still feel vague grating sensations with every chest movement. He could not bring himself to explore the area with his fingers. He could hear a very slight hissing sound with every inspiration and expiration. He was remarkably calm looking at the mess. Calculating. As if looking at a dog that had just been hit by a car.

Carefully he pulled an array of bandages and dressing materials from the shelves. He applied a large mass of gauze swabs to the open wound closing off the skin deficit. As he applied the swabs he could feel the pressure he applied but there was no excruciating pain. Drugs or mind over matter? By holding one end of a self-adhering bandage in his right hand low on his abdominal wall and holding the swabs in place against his chest with his right upper arm he was able to wind a bandage around his abdomen and slowly wind it around his body again and again working up his torso until the gauze swabs were held in place by a firm body bandage extending from his abdomen to his armpits. He then repeated the whole process with more bandages making the entire dressing firm and supportive. With the last few rounds of the body bandage he took the bandage around the back of his neck in an effort to stop the dressing from trying to slide down his torso. Remarkably when finished the pain in his chest was further reduced and his breathing was significantly more comfortable.

He slid his arms back into the sleeves of his overalls and awkwardly pulled the overalls back up over his shoulders and closed the studs.

"As good as new" he stated to himself.

The plan that had been brewing in his head was to exit the building via the outside door to the kennel room, sneak behind the stable block and quickly cross the yard to the back shed and then bolt out of the place in the spare ute. He thought that he would be a sitting duck getting into the Rodeo sitting in the middle of the yard in the wide open. But that had been when the shots were coming from the north side. The last shots had come from the south. Had the shooter moved? How many of the bastards were out there? Would he now be better heading back to the Rodeo as it was protected from the south by the stable block? His mobile phone was in the Rodeo too. Shit. Fucking shit.

The kennel room windows opened out onto the view to the south of the hospital. They were large and you could actually see several kilometres through the sparse scrub. Probably a good option to crawl into the kennel room and try and survey the territory. If he could see nothing then a sprint passed the stable block to the shed might be his safest option.

Between the prep room and the kennel room there was a wooden sliding door. Mick got down on his hands and knees and gently, with his finger-tips, pulled the door open by a few centimetres. No sound. A few more centimetres. No sound. Over a couple of slow minutes he opened the door almost two-thirds of the way open. The door opening would easily be seen by anyone watching from the south. No sound. Had the shooter moved or was he waiting for a clean shot?

Mick crawled through the door on his hands and knees and lay low on the floor of the kennel room. Still nothing. The windows were all shattered and there was broken glass and masonry all over the floor. There were huge holes in the outer wall of the building. From the floor he could see through the holes in the walls to the scrub beyond. By crawling slowly across the floor he got a reasonably unbroken panorama of the scrub. He could see nothing suspicious. No unusual shapes, no glints in the sunlight, no unusual dust clouds…..He stared for several minutes. Nothing.

He turned his head to look back into the kennel room and his guts churned. One dog - a beautiful large German Shepherd called Judge - lay dead in his cage in a huge dark pool of blood. There was blood splattered all over the walls behind him. He lay stiff and in a contorted position with his head bent bizarrely under his body and his limbs extended stiffly behind him on the floor. Christine Elphick's beloved Judge. He had just survived being bitten by a brown snake. Fuck!

In the next cage lay Rocky the obese Staffordshire Bull Terrier which belonged to Smitho and Rosie. He was generally the nicest, waggiest, happiest dog in the entire universe. He was undoubtedly one of Mick's favourite patients. Rocky was back in hospital being treated for yet another bout of pancreatitis most likely brought on by eating too much of Rosie's left-overs from the diner. He'd been in and out of the hospital intermittently over the last 4-5 years as he got fatter and fatter and the bouts of pancreatitis got more frequent and more severe. Talking to

Smitho and Rosie about putting him on a diet and not feeding fatty left-overs was like smacking your head off a brick wall. It made no difference at all to them but gave Mick an excruciatingly sore head. They were going to kill that dog with Rosie's fry-ups.

Rocky was staring at Mick pleading with his eyes. There was no grin, no tail wag, no happy yowling greeting... He looked shocked, pale and miserable. His eyes were imploring for Mick to help him. As Mick surveyed the dog through the cage door he stifled a sickened groan. The dog was lying in a pool of blood also... and both his lower hind limbs were missing below the hocks. Bare bone, ragged tendon and bleeding muscle extended from shredded skin. Mick's nausea returned. His head was numb. He stared in disbelief. Both the dogs' hind limbs had been blown off. Fuck. Fuck... Fuck. Mick wanted to scream. Once again he tasted vomit in his mouth.

Mick slowly crawled back into the prep room. He carefully rose and selected a 20cc syringe and a large hypodermic needle from the boxes on the shelves. He crept back into the office and knelt in front of the desk. He reached into the open safe and pulled out a five hundred ml bottle of Lethalbarb – colloquially known as "Green Dream". The brown glass bottle contained extremely concentrated pentobarbitone with an almost luminous green dye added so that it could not be mistaken for any other drug. He fixed the needle to the syringe and then drew 20mls of dark green fluid from the large bottle. Armed with the loaded syringe he walked back through the prep room to the kennel room door. He awkwardly lowered himself back down onto his hands and knees and crawled slowly back into the kennel room. He stopped in front of Rocky's cage. He carefully opened the cage door and reached in and stroked Rocky's head. The hair on his head was matted with blood and covered in a layer of plasterboard dust.

"Hey buddy – I'm so sorry."

Rocky's eyes stared directly at Mick. They were pleading for help. Shocked and confused.

"I'm going to give you something to make you feel better now mate", whispered Mick.

Mick attached the needle of the green coloured syringe to a giving stopper on the dog's intravenous drip line. He reached further back up the line and closed off the drip line with a small plastic clamp. He then gently squeezed the contents of the syringe into the drip line and the green fluid flowed via an indwelling intravenous catheter into Rocky's circulation. Thank God the IV catheter was still in place. Over the next ten to fifteen seconds the fat dog took two or three deep breaths, his pupils slowly dilated and his eyes became vacant and unseeing. His breathing then slowed and stopped over the next thirty or forty seconds. Mick stared at him for several long moments and felt tears stinging his eyes. He'd known Rocky since he was a whippersnapper. He'd played with him at the servo a million times. He'd even fed him the odd sausage himself when nobody was looking. Everybody in town knew Rocky. Everybody in town fed Rocky. Rocky was everybody's friend. How the hell could he break the news to Smitho and Rosie? They would be devastated. He was their child. And what a ridiculously absurd way to go.

Chapter 12

Mick lay on the floor and stroked Rocky's head. He wondered how on earth he would break the news to Smitho and Rosie. The pain in his own head pulled his thoughts back to his immediate problems. He had to get out of here. He started focusing on the outside door of the kennel room. Surely it was his best escape route. There had been no shots for several minutes. Had the shooter moved again? Was there more than one shooter? He had made a plan. He had to get to the spare ute out in the back shed. If he went out the kennel door he was an easy target from the south. If he went out the back door he had to cross the whole yard and would be an easy target from the north. Once in the shed he would be protected on all sides except the front opening facing the hospital. Surely once in the shed he would be protected until he drove out. Where the hell was the shooter? Was he surrounded? The longer he waited, the more time the shooter had to move again and come even closer. He should stick to the plan and not waste time. He should get moving before the shooter started firing again.

The hair on the back of Mick's neck slowly pricked up. He had heard something outside. Out the front towards the main road. A vehicle. He strained to listen. It had stopped. Silence... After several long seconds he heard a door slam and the crunching of footsteps on gravel. The footsteps became louder as they hit the wooden steps up to and onto the veranda. Suddenly there was loud banging on the front door of the building.

Fuck.

Mick froze. He held his breathe. He expected the front door to explode under rifle fire at any instant.

There was more banging. Someone was shouting. It was hard to make out the words but it was a familiar voice - someone he knew he should recognise.

Mick crawled back into the prep room and got to his feet. The muffled shouting from outside was getting louder. He sidled to the open doorway which led from the prep room into the reception area and waiting room. The banging continued. He carefully peered through the doorway to the front door of the building. Through the patterned glass of the front door he could make out the round bearded figure of "Big George" Richardson, a small time cattle producer from just outside town. Big George's voice boomed.

"Mick – I know you're in there. I saw your truck pull in here earlier. Open the bloody door"

Mick knew he couldn't leave him out there. He would most likely get shot at. But was he involved with the shooting? Fuck? He couldn't be. No way. He was a real nice guy - useless - but real nice. He must be here chasing some vaccine or drugs for the cows.

The whole waiting room and reception area had huge windows looking out onto the road, and to both sides of the building. The front of the building was a bit like a goldfish bowl. If Mick moved into this area he could be a sitting duck for the shooter. But Big George was a godsend. He could be Mick's saviour. Shit. He had to let him in.

"Open the bloody door Mick"

Big George was banging hard enough that he might break the door.

Mick stumbled across the room as fast as his legs would carry him. He pinned himself tightly to the wooden panelling at the left side of the door. The large floor to ceiling vaccine fridge stood two metres away on the right side of the door. The massive fridge gave him reasonable protection from the south facing windows. This could be a relatively safe position. Mick shouted.

"George – Hold on. I'll just unlock the door"

Mick slowly undid the dead bolts and then turned the key in the lock beside the door handle. As soon as the key was turned Big George stormed through the door and slammed it closed behind him.

As Mick stepped away from the wall into Big George's line of vision, the huge man turned to stare at him. His face was bright red and large veins pulsed on his forehead. Trails of white froth and spit matted his greying untidy beard. His dirty checked work shirt strained against his huge gut and the crotch of his sagging track suit pants hung between his knees. He stood with clenched fists shaking violently.

As Mick opened his mouth to speak Big George punched him straight in the side of the head. Mick hit the floor like a sack of spuds. What the fuck? His head, shoulder and chest screamed in pain as Big George laid a size 12 Blundstone boot straight into his abdomen making him curl up like a foetus. The pain was suddenly off the Richter scale again and he found it hard to breathe at all.

Big George was screaming at the top of his voice.

"You fucking little shit. I told you to stay away from my Melanie months ago... You grotty little bastard. Now she's up the duff. Up the fucking duff. What're you gonna do now you smart arsed little prick?"

Mick swung another huge Blundstone boot which struck Mick across both knees.

"I asked you... What the fuck are you gonna do now?"

Mick's brain was trying to unravel what on earth Big George was screaming about. He'd been shot in the chest by whoever the fuck was out there and now this arsehole had come in and belted him in the head... And now he was now mouthing off about Melanie. Melanie??? What the fuck? As the penny slowly began to drop, Mick looked up to meet Big George's bulging red eyes. Then the world began to move in slow motion.

Big George's head exploded. The left side of his face blew off and splattered across the walls and ceiling in a bizarre fountain of blood and smashed tomatoes. Simultaneously he was lifted off the ground and thrown into the glass door of the vaccine fridge which shattered into a million fragments. Shards of broken glass flew around the room dislodging bottles and containers from shelves and slamming into the reception counter. As Big George's twitching body sunk into the remains of the fridge his chest became impaled on the ragged glass on the lower part of the door. Blood poured from the inside of the fridge and soaked across Big George's filthy checked shirt. His arms twitched as if having an epileptic fit and his legs kicked violently for several seconds. His huge chest heaved and harsh gasping, gurgling noises came from where his head used to be. After several excruciating seconds all movement stopped. Bright red blood continued to flow out of the fridge door and form a large red tacky pool around the lifeless torso.

The horrible sweet taste of vomit was once again in Micks mouth. His guts ached. His chest wall was screaming and his head felt like it had been struck though by a pick axe. His brain was functioning however. He had to move. Fuck he had to get out of here.

Chapter 13

Mick rolled onto his stomach and pushed himself across the floor with his legs. His left arm picked a path through the broken glass on the floor and his right arm he held close to his body as any movement of his shoulder caused hellish pain. Mick concentrated on staying low on the floorboards trying to minimize any chance of being seen from outside. Slowly but steadily he inched from the reception area back into the relative safety of the prep room. Once there, he climbed gingerly to his feet and listened intently. There was no noise from outside. None at all. Where was the shooter? The shot that had taken out Big George had come through a window on the north side. The shooter had moved again. Or were there guns on both sides?

If the shooter was still on the north side then any attempt to reach the Rodeo would have Mick out in the open between the back door of the hospital and the vehicle. He would be a very easy target. Even if he made it to the Rodeo he would be a sitting duck in the driver's seat of the vehicle while he started her up.

The silence was broken by more shots accompanied by the noise of glass shattering. The noise came from the general direction of the yard. What was the bastard up to? There were dull metallic thunks as if bullets were tearing through metal and more sounds of glass shattering. Suddenly Mick realised that his would be assassin was shooting up the Rodeo, cutting off his most likely escape route.

Mick crept from the prep room, through the office, to the door which opened to the hallway and the back door. He crouched low by the door and tentatively stole a look down the hallway and through the open back door. He could just see into the yard. The windscreen of the truck bad been completely shot out and fragments of broken glass covered the bonnet. The vehicle shook with each new explosive impact as shot after shot reduced the vehicle to a deformed wreck. The smell of diesel was drifting down the hallway. Mick realised that his previous plan to exit via the kennel room and try to get to the shed and the spare vehicle was his only chance of escape.

Suddenly, in the space of a microsecond, the air in the building was sucked out the back door. In the same instant a blinding flash of orange and white light and a hurricane of superheated air blasted in from the yard. The noise was deafening. Mick was blown away from the doorway of the office back onto the floor. He felt scorching heat burn his face and hands. He thought his eardrums had burst simultaneously and the gross explosion of noise was replaced by a high pitched ringing through his whole head. Pain tore through his chest and head. Fragments of broken wood and masonry flew down the hallway and ricocheted off the walls. The foul smell of burning diesel and paint filled the air.

Fuck it was hard to breathe again. Every breath was painful. Mick's chest hurt like a bastard. He could feel his broken ribs scraping each other, every raw nerve screaming. The pain was excruciating. The air he was breathing in was foul and hot. It tasted of ash and diesel and he was gagging with every breath.

What the fuck? What the fuck was happening?

If he didn't move he was going to die here.

He slowly climbed to his feet using the shelves of his office library as a climbing frame. He could hear nothing apart from a constant ringing. His vision was still blurred by floating shimmering white shapes, but smoke and clouds of black dust made seeing his surroundings even more difficult.

Mick stumbled through the office by feel into the prep room. He had to keep moving. He crossed the prep room and looked into the kennel room from the prep room door. Visibility was a lot better in here. He could see through the broken walls to the outside. There was black smoke lingering in the still morning air.

He had to get out.

He bent low and walked into the kennel room and then down to the door at the far end. There were no shots as he went. Was there no shooter out there? Or was the smoke giving him cover? He looked at the door. This was it – his only way out. He had no idea what lay on the other side. Escape... or suicide? He glanced back at the two dead dogs lying in their cages. His brain was numb.

He whispered "Sorry guys. I'm really so fucking sorry. I'll be back to fix you up later."

Chapter 14

Mick unlocked the back door. He pulled it slowly open. Nothing…. No shots. He stood behind the wall to the side of the open door. He held his breath. The ringing in his head made it impossible to hear anything. He could see the lawn and garden beds behind the stables. Black smoke lingered in the air. Beyond the stables lay the open gravel of the yard which he had to cross to reach the shed. The widest 10 metres of gravel in the world. God it looked a long way across. But he had to get to the gravel to cross it. If someone was still in the paddocks or scrub to the south he would be an easy target in front of the long back wall of the stables. There could be no hanging about.

Mick stepped out the back door and then dropped himself over the edge of the veranda onto the grass below. As his feet hit the ground pain jarred through his upper body and head .There was no time for pain. He was already stooped and running across the grass. He felt like he was moving in slow motion but his head was computing at a millions miles an hour.

"No shots… No shooter this side? Might only be one shooter? Could he stop behind the stable block before crossing the gravel? Maybe just long enough to catch his breath? Maybe the shooter had him in his sights and was waiting for him to stop?"

Mick slowed towards the far end of the stable block. Still no shots. He stooped and crouched low on the grass. No shots. He mustn't hang around long. He was gulping in mouthfuls of gritty smoke filled air. His chest was burning.

He looked across the gravel to the shed. Ten metres of death trap.

Mick took off like Usain Bolt out of the blocks. He was still crouched but sprinting across the gravel. Slow motion again….Each footfall in the gravel and his feet slid away from him sucking the energy out of his legs. It was hard to go in a straight line. His torso weaved to keep balance as his feet splayed out in different directions. He willed his body across the space. He was wading in treacle. His legs were leaden and sluggish. His lungs screamed for air. Every inch took an eternity.

The gravel behind him blew into the air and sharp rocks smacked into the backs of his legs. Fuck – he'd been spotted.

Another shot ripped through the ground under his feet. Shock waves from the bullets hammered his back and legs. Fuck... He was going to die... He somehow managed to push one leg in front of the other and lunged towards the shed. As he flew through the air more gravel exploded underneath him peppering his thighs and groin with violent gravel shards.

He hit the concrete floor of the shed and rolled. The pain as he hit the floor was beyond excruciating. His eyes and head were in agony and he didn't think that he had an intact rib left in his chest. His lungs were on fire.

He had landed between the shed wall and his clutter of heavy farm machinery. Although he could hardly hear he realised that any fresh shots were lost in the mess of tractor trailers, backhoe shovels and other vehicle attachments that he had landed behind. He lay still and prayed again.

Slowly the pain subsided. He was breathing short, shallow breaths again. His vision was improving and he became aware that he could now hear things other than the constant ringing in his ears. He had to move before the shooter moved and got a clean shot at him where he lay. He had to get to the old utility truck at the back of the shed near the granny flat.

Mick got to his hands and knees and crawled between farm implements to the back of the shed. He then crawled along the back wall until he was behind his old Ute. The battered old truck was ancient but he kept it fuelled up and in reasonable nick for the odd day when the Rodeo had to get serviced or had a rare mechanical problem.

Mick got to his feet and tentatively crept along the side of the vehicle to the driver's door. The granny flat kept the ute concealed deep in the back of the shed and out of view from the north side of the property. Quietly he cracked the door and slid into the cab. Mick ignored the pain in his chest and head as he pulled himself into the driver's seat with both arms. It took painful seconds to rescue the ute keys from deep inside the left trouser pocket of his overalls. The damned things were tangled in the blood sodden material of the pocket lining… Pricks… Eventually he had them. Awkwardly he put them in the ignition with his left hand. He lifted his right hand carefully and put his fingers on the keys. He could work his fingers OK. It was just excruciating lifting his arm up and down.

Mick looked out of the windscreen. The yard was unrecognisable. The burning wreck of the Rodeo was pouring black smoke into the sky in front of him. Flames were leaping out of the missing windows and licking around the roof and the bonnet. There was a black ash mantle for several metres around the vehicle's skeleton. The truck was sitting on bare black wheel rims. The back of the Vet Hospital was charred black. Small flames danced from several areas of guttering and on several spots on the veranda. There were several sheets of corrugated iron missing from the blackened roof.

Fuck.

Fuck.

"No time to hang around crying you arsehole." Mick muttered.

He turned the keys in the ignition and simultaneously dropped the clutch and hit the accelerator full tilt. He lifted his right hand onto the steering wheel with his left hand and then shoved the gear lever into first. As he released the clutch the old ute's engine screamed and it flew out of the shed leaving shreds of burned rubber on the concrete behind.

Mick aimed the ute straight at the Vet Hospital between the burning Rodeo and the stable block. The smoking wreck could provide some protection against shots from the north. The vehicle's tyres struggled for traction on the loose gravel and the rear end slid towards the stable block. Mick struggled for control. As the ute straightened he spun a frantic left just passed the wrecked Rodeo and for several long microseconds the old ute faced directly south. Mick thought he might die there and then. He must have been staring straight at his attacker. The moment was in slow motion…Mick scanned the cattle yards and the rugged country beyond but could see no hint of a gunman. In the same moment he half expected it all to end. But no shots came.

Mick then threw a sudden right turn to gain access to the gravel road out of the property. The old vehicle screamed and bit into the gravel. Mick climbed through second and third gears in a matter of milliseconds. As he screeched past the Vet Hospital the windscreen of the old ute exploded in to a million flying glass shards. Without thinking or seeing he threw a big left turn onto the highway rocking onto two wheels. The passenger side wing mirror exploded as a large hole was ripped in the ute's bonnet. As the vehicle straightened and regained traction with all four wheels, the back window exploded sending glass fragments into the back of Mick's head. Fuck. He clung to the steering wheel like a man possessed, cringing with the new onslaught of pain. He sank his foot hard onto the accelerator and the truck fishtailed for 50 or 60 metres leaving more burned rubber on the tarmac. Mick hastily moved through the rest of the gears until he was hurtling north towards town faster than the old ute had ever travelled before.

He had made it to the open road.

He was alive.

He had to fly like bat out of hell to stay alive.

He was desperate to get away.

Fuck he hurt.

What a fucking arsehole of a day…

Chapter 15

It was two straight kilometres to the bridge and the ute was flying. Mick's foot had the accelerator pedal pinned to the metal of the floor. The road ahead was clear.

Mick stared into the cracked remnants of the rear view mirror still fixed to the frame of the shattered windscreen. There were clouds of black smoke pouring into the sky above the vet hospital but the road was empty behind him. He kept focused on the road behind. No vehicle followed. He continued to stare - convincing himself that no-one was following.

Moving his head to get a wider field of vision from the mirror he caught sight of his own reflection. His hair was pasted to his head and coloured red-purple. His eyes were bloodshot. The crow's feet around his eyes made pale cracks in the dried blood which covered most of his face.

He lifted a hand to wipe a lump of stringy pink tissue from his forehead. It stuck to his skin tenaciously. He managed to pick it off and it stuck to the grimy fingers of his left hand. He glanced at the tacky pink tissue and felt the hairs on the back of his neck rise. He suddenly felt extremely cold. Stuck between his fingers was part of Big George's brain.

Jesus Christ....

Jesus H Christ.....

Big George was dead. Fuck. His head had exploded. Fuck. He relived the excruciating. moment in his mind.

Big George was dead. Melanie is pregnant. Fuck. Fucking Fuck. It couldn't be his. Melanie was the town bike. It couldn't be his. He only went there once - in recent memory - in an alcohol drenched haze - after Phoebe Lawrence's wedding. She had raped him...she was out of control...he couldn't get away... But... She had the most fantastic tits he had ever seen. They were truly magnificent... A few months before the wedding, however, he had been quietly knocking Melanie off on Saturday afternoons in the backroom of the hairdressers where she worked, while the rest of Stewarts River were playing or watching sport. It had been a magic way to spend Saturday arvos. That had stopped abruptly when big George had pulled him aside one day in the frozen food isle at the local grocery store and stated, "Stay away from my Melanie or I'll tear your bollocks off..." Mick was fond of his bollocks and took the warning seriously. He'd heard that most of Stewarts Rivers first fifteen had had their hair cut quietly on Saturday arvo since he'd vacated his spot. It could be anyone's. Just not his. Fuck.

Fuck.

The road behind him was still clear. If the shooter knew the area he could be travelling parallel to the highway on the dirt. Mick could see no tell-tale dust clouds in the scrub back towards the Vet Hospital.

The Rankin Bridge over Stewarts River was straight ahead. As he focused on the bridge he suddenly became aware of blue and red flashing lights approaching the bridge from the north. He was still 200 metres from the bridge but could clearly see the police vehicle crossing it and stopping on the road just on the south side. A policeman climbed out of the vehicle and stood waving on the northbound lane. Mick was flying towards the bridge and hit the brakes, his eyes searching the rear view mirror for signs of another vehicle behind him. None.

The battered old vehicle pulled to a halt 2-3 metres from the waving policeman. He was tall and built like a brick shit-house. He looked seriously pissed off. Mick recognised him as Ben Flood – recently separated from Margaret, his wife of 10 years. The gorgeous Margaret...

Mick should have been delighted to find any policeman racing to his aid. But Ben Flood? Fuck, it could have been anyone else. Mick had accidently shagged this man's wife, the most gorgeous Margaret, on numerous occasions during the recent cool winter months. She had the most gorgeous arse and the most beautiful smile. Her little boobs were absolutely delicious. She had the body of a gym junkie. She was fit and exuberant. Man she was incredible... and insatiable... and God did she scream...

Ben had turned up unexpectedly at one of their screaming sessions when supposed to be on patrol 110 kilometres away in Albeston. Margaret and Mick were concentrating hard on one of the more acrobatic positions from the Kama Sutra... page 94... Ben did not appreciate their dedication at all. He blew his stack and went completely berserk. He started smashing bedroom furniture against walls and waving his handgun in both of their faces and screaming like a mad man. He would probably have killed them both if the gorgeous Margaret hadn't hammered him in the head with a gin bottle. It is quite likely that Mick would have suffered his first ever gunshot wound on that night if Margaret hadn't found her weapon on the bedside table. Thank God for gin. Mick had left the scene of the crime before Ben had regained consciousness.

Their paths had not crossed since.

"Get out of the vehicle." The policeman shouted the command.

Mick looked around at the road behind and the scrub to the south but made no attempt to leave the ute.

"Get out of the vehicle now" Ben's hand slid down to his holster where his gun nestled menacingly. He stood silently for a few seconds and then slowly drew the gun out and pointed it directly at Mick through the gaping windscreen.

"Get out of the vehicle... Now."

Mick heard the command despite the ringing in his ears. He was caught between the devil and the deep blue sea. He lifted his left hand and waived in acknowledgement. Slowly he took his right hand off the steering wheel and reached across and opened the door with his left hand. He pushed the door open and slid down onto the tarmac. He stood there behind the door his chest and head getting hammered by a crescendo of pain as he started to make his body move again.

"Round the front of the vehicle," the policeman barked.

As Mick stepped slowly around the door and shuffled to the front of the ute, Ben Flood's posture changed. The muscles in his arms and neck tensed. His hand tightened around his firearm. He had not expected to see Mick in such a state of trauma.

"What's going on Mick?"

"I've been shot. They shot Big George. He's dead." Mick spoke quietly, his head throbbing with every word. "I think it's ISIS. I don't think they're far behind. We should get out of here."

The policeman stared at Mick and considered. There had been reports of an explosion at the vet hospital and reports of shots being fired. After Mick's Internet appearance the local police had been party to a painful number of briefings from the anti-terrorist squad and the army. The INTEL was that ISIS sympathisers could be at large. Maybe he should get this prick out of here and call in the big boys.

Ben Floods shoulder disappeared in a mist of bright red spray as he hurtled over the tarmac crashing into the side of the white police 4WD. An aerosol of red blasted a stunning circular pattern across the windows and white paint. The second impact only a fraction of a second later tore directly through the front of his chest – spraying the mangled remnants of his heart and lungs out through a football sized hole in his back. The beetroot coloured spray flew through the smashed window of the driver's door and spattered across the front seats and windscreen of the vehicle. His body crumpled and folded onto the tarmac. His legs twitched like a demented puppet for less than a second and then all movement was gone. A large pool of blood spread out from below the lifeless form.

Mick's life was again moving in slow motion. He watched Ben Flood's dying moments and realised that his ute was being torn apart by more high powered bullets. The explosions of tearing metal rang through his head. He stooped and started sprinting for the river bank. His legs were leaden and he feared he was going to go down on the tarmac, but his brain screamed and forced his legs to keep pumping. More metallic explosions behind him. He had to reach the river bank. He could hear fizzing noises in the air behind him and he was rocked forward by the shock waves of the invisible bullets he was evading. As he dived for the long grass of the river bank he felt a hellish pain in the top of his head as concrete shrapnel flew everywhere from a bullet impacting on the bridge. He crashed down through the rocky undergrowth. He tumbled 4-5 metres down the steep incline and came to a jarring halt as he hit the dry bedrock at the edge of Stewart's River.

Darkness threatened to engulf him. The world was spinning violently. Loud blinding white lights exploded out of the darkness. Nausea made him retch. Ridiculous pain racked every inch of his battered body. Breathing was impossible. He gasped for air like a drowning man. He had to stay conscious. He could not succumbs to the darkness. He was dead if he let go.

Chapter 16

Mick lay face down on the dry, hard rock of the river bank. He grimaced as he strained to look back up the embankment that he had just fallen down. It was rough and steep. Boulders, scrub bushes and red dirt. He could see neither of the vehicles he had fled from up on the road. The blood spattered police vehicle and his own battered old ute were hidden by the steep incline of the embankment which climbed up to the road and the aged metal-work of the Rankin Bridge. His whole body ached. His head pounded relentlessly.

He could hear no more shots. He calculated that the shooter was unlikely to see him now unless he moved right up to the edge of the embankment. The shots had come from the scrub to the west of the highway. The terrain would be slow to cross. Mick was safe just for the moment, but if the gunman moved close, he would be an easy target.

Should he hide under the bridge? In the scrub? No way – he would be a sitting duck. He would have no way to escape. Should he try and get back to his vehicle while the gunman was likely to be on the move? That was an absurd idea. Going back to the truck would be suicidal. A vision of Ben Flood's torso exploding through driver's window of the police vehicle appeared inside his head. Fuck. No way. His only chance was to get in the river and float downstream. The township of Stewarts River was about two kilometres down river from here. If he could make it to the long left hand bend 200 metres from the bridge he would gain protection from the overhanging trees on the western bank. Then hopefully he could float down into the centre of town where surely somebody could help him. He had no other choice. He couldn't stay here.

As Mick tried to push himself to a standing position his shoulder and head sent horrendous electrical shocks though the rest of his body. The world was spinning. Mick's right arm would not move of it's own volition. He made it to his knees and crawled across the rough red rock using his left arm and his battered legs. His right arm dragged behind. It took several torture filled minutes to cross the 4-5 metres to the water's edge. Once at the edge he crawled into the shallow water where the small, sharp rocks of the river bed cut painfully into his hand and his knees. Once he felt the cool water soak through the chest of his overalls he dropped into the water and pushed away from the shallows with all the remaining strength in his legs.

The water engulfed him. The coolness of the water wrapped around his body. His legs felt no pain. The cool cocoon reduced the pain in his chest dramatically. Within moments his head began to clear and escape from it's nauseous spinning world. He rolled slowly onto his back and stared at a striking clear blue sky. He managed to take long breaths and clear his lungs of residues of smoke and diesel. He could actually taste fresh air.

His work boots had filled with water and his feet were pulling him downwards. By kicking the heal of one boot against the other he managed to remove both boots and send them off into the depths of the river. Having discarded his boots his legs gently floated up towards the surface and he began to drift downstream with minimal effort. Within a few moments he was shaded underneath the Rankin Bridge and watched as the reflections from the water played silently on the underside of the metal support beams and the huge concrete slabs which carried the traffic across the river. Moments later he was out from under the bridge and once again looking into the vast empty blue sky as the river carried him gently north.

He realised that the water in the middle of the river was moving fastest and kicked with his feet so that he moved across into the strongest current about 10 metres from either bank. He floated on his back with his feet pointing back towards the bridge. He was soon 40 or 50 metres from the bridge and with minimal effort was able to scan the bridge and the embankments on either side.

No sign of movement on the bridge. He could just make out the top of the police vehicle on the south side. In the blue sky beyond, a huge, black pall of thick smoke climbed slowly towards the heavens. Stewarts River Veterinary Hospital was probably being incinerated by now. What a fucking waste. It had taken him years to build, years to be able to afford to build, years to accumulate all his gear and years to build the business up. His brain was suddenly going back though his paperwork of the previous few months. His insurance was all up to date wasn't it? Fuck it had better be.

The black smoke would be visible for miles he thought. A funeral pyre for Judge and Rocky. A funeral pyre for Big George. Shit, nobody deserved to die like that. Mick cringed as he saw the grotesquely injured bodies in his head. The poor dogs were a terrible vision. The picture of Big George's lifeless form impaled on the door of the fridge with a lake of blood pouring onto the reception room floor was excruciating.

He dragged his thoughts back to the moment. He scanned the bridge and the riverbanks carefully. No sign of movement. No sign of life at all. So far so good. He kept drifting towards the safety of the river bend.

His focus on the bridge was intense but slowly he began to realise he had new problems. His breathing was becoming painful again and he realised that he was breathing with shorter and faster breaths. Slowly he was beginning to realise that it wasn't such a good idea to be floating in a river with open chest wounds. Maybe he should have thought this through more thoroughly. He realised that the beautiful clear water of the Stewarts River was likely leaking into his thorax via the bullet hole in his chest. Fuck. Maybe he should get out of the river sooner rather than later… Before he filled up and sank…

He was about 150 metres from the bridge and started scanning the banks on either side. He twisted his neck to see the bend in the river behind him. Maybe he should make an early exit if he could see a safe spot on the bank where he could climb out unseen.

His thoughts froze. There was movement on the bridge. A glint of glass or metal reflected in the morning sunlight.

A spurt of water leaped into the air roughly 6 or 7 metres from his feet. A second later a second water spurt blew into the air a metre to the side of his right foot and a stream of white bubbles hissed though the water alongside him.

Mick instantly realised he was being shot at again.

Holy Shit. He felt like a fish being shot at in a barrel.

Immediately Mick turned and duck-dived. Suddenly his chest pain exploded and an invisible mallet struck him between the eyes. It was so difficult to hold his breath. He aimed downstream slanting towards the western river bank. The pain was ridiculous – he had to get air. As he surfaced and gulped for fresh air two more water jets flew into the air a couple of metres away somewhere behind him. He heard hissing in the water below him.

He duck-dived again and swam as hard as he could for the eastern bank. He held his breath until he thought his lungs were on fire. He had to stay down. He had to reach the shore. He had to hold his breath... Eventually he could not swim further. His body was burning with pain. He floated with the current and drifted downstream. He was going to pass out. The world was moving in slow motion again but this time darkness was creeping into his brain.

He broke the surface coughing explosively and gasping for air. He was vaguely conscious of the water hissing around him. He couldn't go down again but he had to. He had to stay alive. His duck - dive was clumsy and shallow but he stayed submerged for another 30-40 seconds. He came up choking and retching raucously. As he gulped in air his feet dragged on gravel. He was in shallow water. He clumsily searched again for the river bed and planted his feet in the small rocks below him. With only his eyes and his nose out of the water he stared back in the direction of the bridge. The bridge was lost from sight. The overhanging boughs of large fig trees on the western river bank blocked his view. He had managed to swim just around the edge of the river bend.

There were no more shots.

He stood in the water breathing through his nose for several minutes. Slowly, very slowly he found his chest stopped burning. The darkness faded from his eyes and his brain. He couldn't move. His brain was numb. His body was in shock.

This was absurd.

He was in a nightmare.

He was in Purgatory.

No - he was in hell.

Chapter 17

Minutes passed and Mick realised that the shooter could be on the highway and heading north. There were paddocks between the road and the river but they were unfenced. Any vehicle could be driven across the paddocks to the trees on the water's edge. He was in no fit state to run or fight. He had to stay in the water and get into town.

Mick gently pushed off into the current and floated north. He stayed close to the trees only 3-4 metres from the river bank. He wasn't travelling as fast as he would in the middle of the river but he believed that he had some protection from the trees if the shooter appeared on the bank. From this distance he could easily scan the river bank for movement.

He floated quietly and smoothly for several hundred metres. He scanned the river bank. He scanned the river – upstream and downstream. No sign of the hunter. Who the fuck was he? Why the fuck was he intent on killing him? What the fuck had he done? ISIS? In Stewarts River? Fuck there were terror cells in Sydney and Melbourne. Maybe they'd thought he'd be an easy target. He had abused the shit out of them. The world had applauded and raised him up on a pedestal for all to see... For fuck sake...

He realised once again that his breathing was changing. Each breath was laboured. Whether he breathed in short or long breaths he still couldn't get enough air into his lungs. He felt like he was suffocating. He was finding it hard to concentrate. His body felt heavy. His arms and legs like dead weights. A couple of times he gulped in water and then thrashed about coughing. The thrashing made him more tired. He was having problems staying afloat.

Deep in his brain the neurons were still working. He knew he had a punctured chest. He knew he was taking in water. He knew that the water was compromising his lung capacity. He probably had a collapsed lung anyway. If his mediastinum was intact surely he could survive with only one functioning lung. If... The high powered bullets that had blown Ben Flood apart could have torn his mediastinum to shreds... But probably not. He was still alive. He knew that he had to get out of the water before he lapsed into unconsciousness. He was never going to make it to town.

He searched the broad expanse of river extending towards the Stewarts River township. He could just make out the purple haze of the Jacaranda trees in full bloom in the memorial park. The park that was just about to be re-named in honour of his father – "Andrew Gallagher Park". It was all to happen in two weeks, during the Jacaranda festival. His father had loved the park. He had planted many of the Jacarandas there himself. It would be a fitting tribute. The annual Jacaranda Festival in Stewarts River was a highlight in the town calendar. A week of street parties, music, rodeos and sporting competitions. The finale of the festivities, "The Jacaranda Ball", was held on the third Saturday of September, rain, hail or shine. The whole town came out in all their finery and danced in the town hall till the wee hours of the next day. Jacaranda Ball nights were legendary. The drinking, the dancing and the romance... Mick had proposed to Fiona at the Jacaranda Ball. He had bent down on one knee in the middle of the dancefloor and had proposed to the most beautiful woman in creation, in front of the whole town. Shit that had been a long time ago... In another life... The Jacarandas were in full bloom again, but were probably still a kilometre away. Too far. Way too far. He'd never make it.

As he stared at the distant purple haze a white shape extending out from the river bank trees about a hundred metres downstream on his left came into focus. It was a jetty belonging to one of the houses on the outskirts of town. Despite his head spinning and throbbing he recognised it as Chowdry's jetty – the jetty where he'd spent many long summers days, fishing and swimming and pulling kids on biscuits behind the tinny.

Only a hundred metres or so. He could make it.

Chowdry had been Mick's best friend for the best part of the last 20 years. Chowdry had been brought up in Delhi in India where most of his family still lived. He had come to Australia to study Medicine at Sydney University. After 5 years at uni he applied to do his rural training in

Stewarts River in a country practice gaining an excellent reputation in the medicine world due mostly to the stewardship of one Andrew Gallagher – also a Sydney University graduate. Chowdry and Mr Gallagher senior took to each other immediately. They had the same drive for perfection, the same drive to perform state of the art medicine, the same drive regards work ethic and the same social conscience. They both wanted to look after everyone – young or old, rich or poor, privately or publicly funded – it didn't matter for this pair. They wanted the whole community to thrive.

Inevitably Mick and Chowdry soon were introduced and became smitten with each other immediately. Both were young professionals with common interests – medicine - both human and veterinary, travelling, the other sex and a love of alcohol. A full blown bromance ensued. They worked hard and partied hard. They shared a house together for the best part of a year. They dated together and they holidayed together. Before they married their spouses, they were inseparable.

Chowdry met Beatrice Langman within twelve months of arriving in Stewarts River. Beatrice was the daughter of very wealthy grazier whose family owned a huge cattle empire. Their ancestors had arrived in the area just about five minutes after Logan Stewart. Beatrice was the youngest daughter of the Langman clan with two older brothers and two older sisters. She was stunning to look at – voluptuous and beautiful, and was effervescent, vibrant and extremely intelligent. She had just returned to Stewarts River after three years studying journalism in Melbourne and then working for several women's magazines including "Woman's Day" and "Vogue". She had returned to Stewarts River after a dramatic break-up with her fiancé who had been caught sleeping with Beatrice's boss. Beatrice met Chowdry on the rebound. They met at a hospital gala night and fell in love immediately. They were engaged twelve months after they met, and married nine months after the engagement. Mick had been best man at Chowdry's wedding and Chowdry had reciprocated at Mick's. With the arrival of kids – three daughters for Chowdry and Beatrice and one for Mick and Fiona the families had stayed very close and spent many holidays together, babysat for each other and looked after each other kids as if they were all siblings.

Chowdry the prick was in India. He'd been spending weeks at a time there since the start of his marital problems. He was working like a FIFO – fly-in fly-out. He'd fly into town and work at the hospital for a couple of weeks and then fly back to India. Mick was fairly sure he didn't stay at home on these visits. He and Beatrice were always at one another's throats. Mick didn't know if he stayed at a motel or if he bunked down at the hospital. He and Chowdry had spent hours and hours over too many beers and gins discussing where it had all gone wrong. He was the most loyal husband. He loved Beatrice more than life itself. He was a great father. He had never put a foot wrong. But she wanted something else...something more... He had no idea what. His idea of spending time in India was to let her see what life was like without him. Surely she would miss him. Surely she would want him back. Surely.

Like a good friend Mick had visited Beatrice while Chowdry was overseas. He intended to find out why Chowdry had fallen from grace... to find out what on earth the problem was and help his best mate win his wife back again. On the first visit she had cried her eyes out and babbled a whole pile of drivel about true love and kindred spirits. On the second visit after a couple of very large gin and tonics they had dragged each other to bed and shagged until the sun came up. Mick had been a regular visitor after that. He loved counselling sessions. He wasn't too sure if Beatrice and Chowdry would ever get back together though.

Did he feel bad about shagging his best mate's wife?

She was a big girl. She knew what she was doing.

Mick's head was spinning. The black clouds were moving in again. With excruciating effort he tried to control his drift so that he would float alongside the jetty and be able to grab on to one of the submerged concrete pylons or even better onto the ladder which extended down from the jetty deck into the water. Paddling with his left arm only was difficult and his leaden legs were becoming more a hindrance than a help. He focused on the nearest corner of the jetty. He couldn't miss. If he did he wouldn't make it much further.

His body slammed into the corner pylon of the jetty. His chest was hammered against the concrete and air was blasted from his lungs by the sudden force. His head spun and the pain in his chest soared to new heights. His vision failed. He could only see black clouds. He wrapped his arms around the pylon and hung on for dear life. His thighs wound around the pylon too and he crossed his ankles over one another on the far side. He was not letting go.

Mick held himself there for several minutes. His head slowly cleared. He concentrated on breathing short and steady breaths. He ignored the pain. The ladder was two metres away. He couldn't miss it. He slowly lifted his left arm out of the water and grabbed hold of the jetty deck. He could not raise his right arm to do the same. He wriggled around the pylon and crept his left arm along the deck towards the ladder. When he let go with his legs he had to keep hold of the deck with his left hand or he would float away. He focused hard and let go of the pylon with his legs. His body floated past his extended left arm which held fast. He fished for the submerged part of the ladder with his legs. After frustrating seconds he hooked his right leg through the rungs of the ladder. He then let go of the deck and was carried into the ladder by the current. He now clung to the ladder with all his remaining strength.

He was spent. He could not summon the energy to climb from the water. His arms and legs were dead weights. He felt like he had a machete stuck deep in his head, and his chest was begging for mercy. He hung onto the rungs of the ladder as if he was welded on. For several minutes he focused on breathing. His body and brain craving oxygen.

As brain function slowly returned he knew that if he did not get out of the river now he was going to drown there.

With every part of his body screaming at him to stop and give in, he forced his legs to push his body up the ladder and crawled onto the jetty deck. He collapsed flat. He had nothing left. Pain and darkness engulfed him.

The darkness was alive. It crept into his very pores. It insinuated itself deep within the recesses of his brain... Deep within his soul... It silently stole his will to awaken. It wanted him to surrender... Somewhere he sensed there was an elusive light - a light that could lead him back to consciousness and life. He could hear distant voices. They cried and screamed while the elusive light ebbed further from his senses. His father's voice screamed for mercy and his severed head floated in the darkness before him. The darkness became the darkest red and his father's head became Big George's head exploding immediately in front of him. He struggled to move in a torrent of Big George's brains...They stuck to his face and limbs and tightened around his chest restricting his breathing...strangling him slowly... Big George transformed into Ben Flood... The policeman, with most of his chest missing, wanted to kill Mick Gallagher because he had shagged his wife... Margaret was beautiful and calling for Mike to climb into the light but when he finally saw her she was naked and pregnant and looked just like Melanie but her head was exploding like a watermelon sending brain mush and blood throughout the whole universe...

Chapter 18

The pain in his head was excruciating. Every breath hurt. The hard wood of the jetty pushed into every painful contour of his body. Mick couldn't open his eyes. Too sore. Too bright. Too nauseous.

Someone was screaming. The screaming was getting louder. Mick wished it would go away.

"Mick, Mick ... Talk to me..."

"What have you done...? Speak to me Mick...Speak to me... "

He felt his head being lifted from the rock hard, evil jetty. Softness was pushed under his head.

He slowly opened his eyes and found the beautiful face of Beatrice Chowdry bent over his. Tears were pouring out of her eyes and cascading across the most beautiful skin in the world.

Mick wondered if she was an angel.

"Mick... Mick... Talk to me... Stay with me... "

She gently stroked his face.

"My God Mick... What on earth happened?"

He tried to answer but barely a gasp made it's way through his lips"

He stared at the face above his. God she was beautiful. Perfect eyes. Perfect lips. Perfect teeth. She had to be an angel.

"Did you crash your truck Mick? Did you go through the windscreen? You're face and head are an absolute mess... How did you get in the river? How on earth did you get onto the jetty? Jesus Christ Mick... What on earth have you been doing?"

She paused and waited for a response. None came. His eyes were bloodshot, his skin was pale and cold. His overalls were blood soaked. He was beginning to shiver uncontrollably. He looked like death warmed up. She was genuinely worried that each breath could be his last.

"Mick... Listen... Can you get up? We've got to get you to hospital... You're in a mess... We've got to move you...OK?"

He stared back at her and the semblance of a smile formed on his white lips.

She put her arms slowly under his back and gently lifted him to a sitting position. The pain of moving was excruciating. His head was exploding. With every breath he felt his broken ribs crunching and screaming in protest.

Beatrice's beautiful brown eyes were staring into his. There were small dark brown flecks in the hazel of her irises. Stunning eyes. Hypnotic eyes.

"Now sit here. Don't try to move. I'll back the four wheel drive down to the jetty here. We'll get you on board and then get you to hospital as quick as we can."

She stared at his face imploring him to respond in some way. He blinked both eyes very slowly and deliberately, and returned her stare. His head nod was only slight but the message it conveyed was that he understood. Her heart raced.

She stood and waited a second to check that he could stay sitting up without her support. He winked at her slowly. She smiled back and then departed - running up the slope of the lawn and between the trunks of the old gnarled she-oaks towards the house.

Mick knew he wasn't well. He knew that he should have been dead. He knew that his body was mangled. The pain was incessant. None-the-less he still managed to admire the exquisite curve of her arse in her wranglers as it bounced it's way across the grass. My god that was an exquisite arse... The perfect arse...

The pain was pulling back a little. Breathing was slightly easier sitting up. Feeling was slowly coming back to his arms and legs. He sat and stared into the she oaks. He concentrated on every breath. The air felt better here. Clean and cool.

As the bright morning sunlight glinted between the leaves of the overhead trees he suddenly became uncomfortable and started squinting into his surroundings. The glint of reflected sunlight from the bridge had alerted him to the gunman about to open fire earlier in the morning. How close was he now? Had he tracked him to the jetty or the garden? Was he, even now, in the cross-hairs of telescopic sights? The bright sparkling sun shining haphazardly through leaves made him uncomfortable. He shrank lower again towards the jetty and scanned the surrounding undergrowth for any sign of a hidden marksman.

He heard the roar of the Land Cruiser before he saw it. The square blue vehicle reversed at speed between the gnarled grey tree trunks and down to the bottom of the garden. It came to an abrupt stop a metre from the jetty path.

Beatrice jumped out of the driver's seat. Her wet, bloodstained shirt clung to the curves of her voluptuous body. She swept long, black, shiny hair from her face as she hurried back onto the jetty and knelt in front of Mick.

"Stay still," she advised. "This could be uncomfortable to begin with but it should help slow the bleeding."

She gently placed a cold, wet tea towel wrapped around an ice brick on the back of his head and held it there staring into his eyes. He admired her gorgeous eyes - beautiful despite the redness and the tears still welling in them.

"My God – I thought you were dead."

She bent into his face and kissed him full on the lips. The taste was spearmint and cherries. His brain was functioning bizarrely. He couldn't feel his right arm at all. The pain in his head was off the Richter scale - but he could taste spearmint and cherries.

As she pulled back and looked at him he was presented with the most wonderful view down the front of her shirt. The most beautiful, full, round boobs in the universe - restrained by expensive, black, silk lingerie. Her skin soft and lightly tanned with a smattering of delightful, tantalising freckles. For a moment there was no pain.

"Mick – where does it hurt most? Are you OK to try and move?"

When he did not respond her anxiety rose another level.

She held his head gently but firmly and looked directly into his eyes. His eyes did not meet hers. He seemed focused beyond her face.

"Mick. Do you understand what I'm saying?"

His voice croaked when it eventually came.

"Just enjoying the view… "

A broad grin of realisation lit up her face.

"My God – you're almost dead and you've still got the energy to perv!"

She laughed and choked simultaneously, as a million tears ran down her face and nose.

"I think I'm getting a stiffy" he croaked.

Beatrice laughed and choked and coughed some more.

"You'll die from low blood pressure if you get one of them…" She laughed until she choked again.

She postured so his view improved even more. Maybe he was in heaven. The beginnings of a smile creased the dried blood around his mouth. She stooped in close and kissed him on the forehead.

"We've got to get you in the wagon." She stated. "Probably easiest to open the back door and lift you in there. You can lie on the blankets. Probably easier than trying to get you up and into a seat. You'll probably be more comfortable there too."

Mick nodded slowly and his brain throbbed horribly with the movement.

Beatrice rose and pulled the back door of the vehicle wide open. She then walked round behind Mick. She crouched down and gently pushed both of her arms under his arms and around to front of his chest where she clasped her hands together tightly.

"One, two, three..." She lifted gently and Mick forced his legs under his body and managed to push himself to his feet. The pain in his head and chest returned horrendously. He staggered sideways but Beatrice held him firmly while his head spun and he tried to control waves of nausea. The pain was immense. His vision was obliterated by flashing white lights.

After a few seconds she steered him the few steps along the jetty path, to the vehicle, where he collapsed through the open back door into the compartment behind the back seats. He cried alarmingly as he hit the mass of blankets Beatrice had arranged there. Beatrice cringed and cried out loud herself, "Oh Fuck... Oh fuck... God I'm so sorry Mick..."

Beatrice gently lifted his legs and shoved them into the cramped space as delicately as she could. She grimaced more as he groaned with the movement of each limb.

She was shaking uncontrollably as she bent and kissed the side of his head.

"Just hang in there... Won't be long now... It might be a bit bumpy for the first few minutes. I'll take it as easy as I can."

When Mick did not reply she decided just to put her plan into action and get him to Stewarts River Base Hospital ASAP.

As she slammed the back door shut, the vibrations sent Mick's battered body into gross muscle spasms. He retched painfully and brought up several thousand litres of the Stewarts River.

Chapter 19

The first couple of minutes in the back of the Land Cruiser were like being on a fairground ride during a hurricane. Mick was thrown from side to side of the back compartment of the vehicle, and simultaneously up and down with no gravity one moment and then suddenly the force of 10G's hammering him onto the floor. The nausea was absurd and he vomited till he thought his guts would come out. This was worse than the worst sea-sickness. He prayed for it all to end. Death had to be better than this. He felt pain in every organ, every muscle, every cell of his body. He was sure that every abdominal viscus had been mashed to a pulp and that his bladder and kidneys had ruptured and that death would have been way more acceptable. He knew that he had no lungs left as every inch of his being was screaming for oxygen. Despite his gasping and desperate sucking for air his respiratory efforts were all in vain. He was slowly suffocating. He was fucked. He just wished somebody would switch the off button.

It took several minutes for Beatrice to drive the Land Cruiser out of her property and onto the tarmac on the outskirts of Stewarts River. As she left the property, at just under the speed of light, and turned right onto Masons Road, the backend of the vehicle slid just too far across the road. It smashed through the entrance gate of Greg Puttance's property and obliterated his mailbox. Beatrice was only vaguely conscious that something had struck the backend of the vehicle. Whatever had happened, she would have to sort it out sometime later. She was on a mission. Once on the tarred road, her focus was to get to the hospital with utmost speed…Bugger other traffic, bugger speed limits, bugger road signs and bugger gates and mailboxes. She was a desperate woman. Mick was almost dead in the back. She was getting him to the hospital fast.

Speed had not been the only factor in the destruction of Greg Puttance's gate and mailbox. As the Land Cruiser exited the Chowdrey property several high powered bullets had ripped through the backend of the vehicle entering through the main panel of the back door and then blasting massive holes in the left back side panel and smashing the side panel window as they exited again. The power of the blasts threw the vehicle into the neighbour's entrance gate. The bullets had been deflected by metalwork within the back door panel and had veered from their original trajectory. If they had not ricocheted off the metal struts within the door panel then Mick would have been dead. His wish to meet his maker would have been granted in that very instant. His broken body would have been blown apart. The beautiful Beatrice would have exploded over the steering wheel of the truck. Death would have been instantaneous for both. Fate had favoured them. Neither had seen the vehicle sitting off the tar a hundred metres further down Masons Road. Neither had seen the gunman lying in the undergrowth with telescopic sites focused on the exit from the Chowdrey property. Neither had realised that the smashing of the rear end of the vehicle had been, in most part, caused by shots from a hidden killer.

Greg Puttance was going to be pissed off. He was the local dentist and his property on Mason's Road was his pride and joy. He'd spent months fixing up the entrance to his beloved estate and had flown the elaborate letterbox in from Italy for his wife's birthday. He was a very romantic guy. Beatrice's driving skills would get the blame for the wrecked gate and mailbox, but the bullets embedded in one of the gate posts and in the surrounding trees could tell a different story.

The ride to Stewarts River Base Hospital took less than five minutes once outside the Chowdry property, but for Mick it was an eternity. He felt electric shocks through his head and chest with every pothole and speed hump along the road. He didn't dare to try and move to another position. Air blasted at him from the holes torn in the side panel by the high velocity bullets. Mick thought the air-conditioning was broken. The slightest movement caused insane pain everywhere. The world was spinning and nausea caused him to retch incessantly.

He was vaguely aware that Beatrice was talking during the trip. Was she trying to keep him awake or was she on the phone? Mick didn't care. He just wanted the pain and the nausea to stop.

Only moments ago he had been in heaven with a tantalising view of the most perfect breasts in the history of the world.

Life was so cruel.

Now he was sure he'd been banished to Hell...

Chapter 20

The Land Cruiser lurched to a halt in the ambulance bay at the small country hospital. Beatrice leaned on the horn and the noise was deafening. A doctor, two nurses and a paramedic ran from the building within seconds, and headed straight for the back door of the Land Cruiser. The paramedic was pushing a long metal trolley with bed linen on top in the wake of the other three medics. Beatrice jumped out of the vehicle and started shouting hysterically at them all.

"Quickly for Christ's sake...He's dying... He needs blood...He needs pethidine...He needs x-rays..." Beatrice's lovely face was pale and contorted with anguish. She continued to bark instructions...

"Get him inside quickly...He's dying... Get him some blood... Don't let him die...Oh please don't let him die..."

A stocky, red-haired, female nurse pulled open the back door of the truck and the doctor leaned in to the interior to assess the situation. He was twenty-six years old and looked fourteen. He was skinny with thick milk bottle glasses, had dark greasy hair and had a small amount of bum-fluff on his top lip which he thought looked like a moustache. This was his country medicine internship. He'd been assured that he would spend his days checking old ladies arthritic hips with the occasional finger to stitch up from the local abattoir. He'd planned on having a quiet time in the country with hopefully the odd bit of sexual adventure thrown in. In the big city hospitals he never stood a chance with the nurses. The better looking, faster talking guys always beat him into second place. In the country maybe he'd be a bigger fish in a smaller pond. So far he'd scored some heavy petting and a hand-job at a nurse's party, from a skinny chick who said her father was the local vet. He thought he'd arrived in heaven. Then she'd gone back to uni in Sydney leaving him all on his lonesome again.

Dr Adrian Kirkton had never, ever intended to work in Emergency. He wanted a quiet life. He thought of himself as a budding geriatrician or maybe even an epidemiologist. The man in front of him had come from a war zone. This wasn't in the brochure.

The bloodied form was in deep shock. Blood-covered and shivering. The colour of his mucous membranes was almost cyanotic, never mind pale. He had bleeding wounds on his head and face and a ragged blood soaked tear in his overalls high on his right chest. The overalls were absolutely covered in blood. Surely it was not all from this patient.

"We need to get him inside ASAP," stated the young doctor. "We need IV fluids and a cross match as quick as we can. We need plasma expanders and mannitol. We need cannulas in both arms and prep his lower limbs also."

The younger, slightly built, fair haired nurse turned and sprinted back into the building.

"Right Charlie," the young doctor continued as he glanced at the male paramedic with pock marks all over his face and a severe grey crew-cut, "let's slide him onto a board and then we can lift him onto the trolley."

Without hesitation Charlie produced a long orange plastic board from under the trolley. It was about 2 metres long and 60 centimetres wide with slits cut just inside the edges all the way round turning the edges into handles. The doctor and the red-haired nurse moved out of Charlie's way. He placed one narrow end onto the floor of the compartment in the back of the truck where Mick lay groaning and held tightly to the other end. The end inside the truck was positioned near Mick's head and Charlie pushed the other end of the board as close as he could to Mick's feet, but on the outside of the door. Both the young doctor and the red-haired nurse leaned over the top of the board and gently grabbed handfuls of Mick. The Doctor nodded to the nurse, "OK Leanne – we'll move him on three... one, two, three..." On the doctor's command they both gently but firmly pulled Mick over onto his back and onto the rigid board.

Mick cried pitifully as he was manhandled and then slumped flat on the board. He was shivering uncontrollably and still retching. Excruciating pain racked his body and hammered into his head. Mick now had no idea where he was or what was going on.

Dr Kirkton and Nurse Leanne grabbed a corner of the board each up near Mick's head, and with directions from Charlie the whole board was lifted out of the back of the Land Cruiser and onto the waiting trolley. Charlie quickly and efficiently strapped the board to the trolley and the three members of the team pushed the trolley smoothly up a short ramp at the front of the ambulance bay and through a plastic-curtained door into the hospital.

Beatrice was now sobbing uncontrollably and clung to the side of the trolley as it moved. She'd brought Mick this far and she wasn't leaving him until she knew all was well. The Land Cruiser was left idling in the ambulance's spot with both front doors wide open and the back door gaping wide.

Inside the hospital Mick could see the ceiling lights passing by and blurred signs on walls passing also. Several people came to stare as he passed. They may have talked to him – he could see their mouths moving but could hear no words. These visions only managed to heighten his nausea. He continued to retch.

When the trolley came to a halt he could actually hear muffled voices. Several stethoscope heads hovered above him. Several hands moved his arms and legs and the pain made him groan loudly. The guy with the glasses talked to him a lot. He talked to the others a lot too. He could hear the words... Just couldn't put them together.

He was aware of sharp pricks in his arms.

After these the world went warm and fuzzy.

He could take nice long breaths. At last... Just magic...

The pain slowly left... No more pain. Oh Yes... God this was good...

All he could see now were Beatrice's naked breasts... They were wonderful...

Chapter 21

About an hour after Mick had left the servo Smitho had noticed plumes of thick, black smoke billowing into the air about four or five kilometres south of town. He'd assumed that there'd been a motor vehicle accident and wandered into his office to listen in to the police radio messages on his radio scanner. This was normal behaviour for anyone who owned a tow-truck business. If the police were heading to a prang it was a good option to follow them and tout for business. One of his employees was a very good panel beater.

Smitho knew from an earlier message that several police were already on their way to Albeston to investigate a break in at the bottle shop overnight. He'd heard that more than thirty minutes ago. That meant they'd be gone for two and a half to three hours. That should still leave at least three or four police cars in and around town.

Smitho stared through the window at the rising smoke. It certainly looked like a diesel explosion. He absently checked the EFTPOS machine again as he waited on any police calls. Bloody thing was still out of action. Shit. Most of the regulars would be fine but any out of towners might be put out when he informed them – cash sales only.

After a couple of minutes the radio crackled and the gruff voice of Senior Sergeant Dean Brody came over the airways.

"Calling all cars... Calling all cars... Please respond... We have an explosion reported in the vicinity of Stewarts River Veterinary Hospital 4.1 kilometres south of Stewarts River on Stewarts River Road. Address Number 4016 – repeat 4016... property on the west side of the road. Gunshots reported before explosion... Repeat gun shots reported before explosion... Do we have any takers please?"

Within seconds a reply came in.

"This is car 271, repeat car 271 – Constable Flood. Am abandoning RBT duties on Fotheringham Street and heading to 4016 Stewarts Road forthwith."

Dean Brody responded, "Thanks Ben – I'll get back up out ASAP… Will hold SES and Fire Services until you give all clear re firearms."

"Thanks Dean – copy that."

Smitho was stunned. He stared at the black smoke and wondered out loud. "What the fuck is happening now Mickus?"

Smitho picked up his mobile from the office desk. He walked to the window and stared at the smoke. It looked thicker and blacker than a moment ago. He hit Mick's mobile number… "This phone is not in service…" came the robotic telecom voice. He hung up and hit the number for Stewarts River Veterinary Hospital in his contact list. That phone was dead.

Smitho stared at the smoke in brooding silence. Eventually he murmured to himself, "I might just have to take the tow-truck for a wander down there in a minute…"

Suddenly Police Vehicle 271 screamed past the servo at high speed, siren wailing and blue and red lights flashing wildly. It was a large, white Toyota four wheel drive with blue checks down the side and orange stripes on the tailgate. Smitho watched as the speeding vehicle disappeared down the long straight of the road south towards the Rankin Bridge. He was flying…

"Behave Ben… You'll get arrested if you drive at that speed…" Smitho sniggered to himself. "I might just give you a couple of minutes to suss the situation and then I'll get in the old tow-truck and come and have a looksee…"

Smitho wasn't too excited by the statement about the gunfire before the explosion. Lots of locals shot rabbits and wild pigs at any old time of day. He just hoped that Mick hadn't taken a pot shot at something and hit one of his medical gas cylinders at the side of the vet hospital. That would be a bit exciting…

For the next 15-20 minutes Smitho was busy with a steady stream of customers fuelling up. All were interested in the smoke stack but none of them had driven past. Some thought it would be a car smash, others thought it could be a deliberate scrub burn-off at this time of year. No one seemed overly worried. In a gap in the traffic he strolled up to the entrance to "Rosie's Diner", his eyes fixed on the smoke plume all the way. He stuck his head in the door and let the doorbell ring until Rosie looked up from her smoking hot plate.

When she saw him she wiggled her boobs at him and shouted over her sizzling hash browns.

"You OK my gorgeous hunk of manhood?"

He replied over the heads of customers engrossed in Sunday papers, coffee and steaming hot food.

"Looks like there's been a prang down towards Mick's place. I'm gonna take the tow-truck down for a quick investigate. Can you keep an eye on the servo?"

"Sure will Hot-Stuff. Make sure and take your phone. Let me know if you'll be straight back."

"No worries my little Barbie-Doll of the West..."

Rosie's face lit up with a huge grin. She loved being likened to Barbie. She shouted back at the top of her voice. "Love you Ken."

"Love you too darling..." Smitho grinned back. He blew her a kiss and quietly closed the door leaving Rosie and her wobbling boobs tending lovingly to a grill full of sizzling sausages.

Chapter 22

Smitho pulled out onto Stewarts Road, the main road heading south out of town. The old truck was as noisy as hell and spewed it's own trail of black diesel smoke behind it. Smitho loved the truck. He loved the noise and the vibrations which shook the cab continuously. He loved the oily, diesel smell. He even loved the fact that it was hard to handle and difficult to manoeuvre. He'd owned it for 20 years. It was a work horse. It had done thousands of crash pick-ups. It was a good friend. Smitho felt at home whenever he sat in it.

He moved slowly through the gears and eventually the vehicle gained momentum and began to hurtle down the road like a runaway train. Smitho found this exhilarating. He loved being in control of almost five tonnes of powerful machinery.

About a kilometre and a half out of town the Rankin Bridge came into view as he took the long left bend after the straight. He could see the bridge across the paddocks which led to the river bank. Something was odd. He could see the police vehicle which had roared out of town earlier, lights still flashing, sitting just over the bridge. There was another vehicle parked a few metres in front of it.

Smitho eased the brakes and dropped a couple of gears, and slowed his juggernaut to roughly 40-50 kilometres per hour as he proceeded around the long bend and towards the bridge. As the road straightened and he looked directly down the road and across the bridge he could see the police vehicle at a standstill in the left lane just on the other side of the bridge and no more. An old white ute blocked the right lane facing towards town.

Smitho began to feel uneasy. As he crept closer he could see no sign of anyone around the vehicles nor could he see anyone in the vehicles. The front end and the windscreen of the old ute were smashed to buggery. There was a pile of material or blankets of some sort lying crumpled on the road and pushed up against the side of the police truck. Occasionally a black piece of material on top of the heap got caught in the beginnings of a breeze and tried to blow away.

Smitho grew more uncomfortable the closer he got to the bridge. He crept to the north side of the bridge and stopped. He stared at the vehicles only 30 metres away. The black material flapped on the ground. He realised that there was broken glass all around the police vehicle. A sudden realisation made his guts lurch. He recognised the old ute. It was Mick's. Smitho sat and stared for a full minute. Nothing stirred except the black material waving occasionally when the breeze took it.

The smoke cloud filled most of the sky on the other side of the bridge. It looked like a mushroom cloud moving in slow motion. The black cloud had now spread several hundred metres into the sky, and had crept poisonously across the whole horizon.

Smitho killed the tow-truck engine and the hiss of the air brakes lingered in the sudden silence. He climbed out of the cab and stood in the middle of the road. He couldn't understand what he was seeing.

He called across to the vehicles. "Hello... Is there anybody there?... Hello... Hello..."

Smitho could hear his own heartbeat in the silence that followed.

Slowly he started to walk across the bridge. He kept his focus on the vehicles and kept calling, "Hello... Is there anybody there?"

He was about two thirds of the way across the bridge when he realised that the road between the two vehicles was stained with black fluid. Must be diesel...

He continued onwards slowly. His senses were straining for movement or sound. There was a faint odd buzz in the air but the only movement was the occasional ripple of the black material on top of the heap of blankets leaning against the police four wheel drive.

Suddenly Smitho froze on the spot. He held his breath. He stared intensely at the heap of "blankets". Extending from the heap were two large black boots... He was suddenly extremely cold... right to his core. He realised the blankets were crumpled dark blue policeman's trousers. The trousers were attached to a crumpled purple shirt. A blood streaked arm extended from the purple shirt and disappeared under the police vehicle. Smitho realised that the policeman who'd been driving the truck was lying motionless beneath a black sheet on the bare bitumen. The pool of "diesel" which stained the road between the two vehicles was actually blood emanating from under the sheet.

Smitho's immediate instinct was to turn and run but he couldn't. He could not move. He was trembling and staring at the bloodied arm. He could hear his own heart beating faster than ever before. He could hear his blood pulsing in his veins. He could hear blood pulsing through his brain. He couldn't turn away. He knew he had to help this injured man in whatever way he could. Was he alive or was he dead? He had to know. He couldn't run like a coward and leave a dying man. He had to try and save him.

He walked on slowly. He forced every step. He was determined not to turn away. He had to see under the black sheet. Blood spread out around the crumpled form like a huge halo. It was red and shining around the edges of the sheet and black and dull as it crept away from him and got lost in the road surface.

Smitho stopped beside the man's huge black boots. They were spattered with bright red blood spots. His dark trousers looked wet and his legs protruded from under the black sheet at impossible angles. The black sheet had thin crinkled white lines in multiple areas but most of the areas which should have been white were now dark red. Small pools of congealed red blood had collected in the folds of the sheet.

Smitho's gaze was drawn to the driver's door of the police vehicle above the blood covered figure. The door panel was caved in with blood from top to bottom. Shards of red glass sat in the sills where the window should have been and blood and shredded meat were spread across the whole of the front of the inside of the vehicle. The windscreen, the dashboard and the steering wheel were drenched in thick red blood. It looked as if someone had thrown a bucket of thick, lumpy, red paint straight through the driver's window.

Sporadically the blue and red lights on top of the truck spun and flashed bathing the scene in bizarre coloured strobe light.

Smitho glanced at the other vehicle. Where the fuck was Mick? Was he lying somewhere like this too? Fuck...

He had to look under the sheet. He knew the guy had to be dead. He knew it had to be Ben Flood. He knew that if the injured policeman was alive at this point and he did nothing to try and help him he would torture himself mentally for the rest of his life. He had to look. He had to help if he could. He just had too.

He steeled himself. He took several deep breaths and knelt by the policeman's feet. He grasped the bottom right corner of the sheet with his left hand. It had been trapped or wrapped under the policeman's left boot. In one movement he lifted the sheet and unwound it from around the man below. The vision which was unveiled was hideous.

Ben Flood's trousers were soaked in blood. The front of his chest was gaping open through the mangled material of his shirt. Hundreds of buzzing black flies erupted from the gaping chest wound as the sheet was moved. Hundreds more stayed to feast on the mangled tissue which was exposed – broken ribs, cartilage, lungs and shredded airways. Smitho imagined he could see gravel deep within the wound...or was he looking at the road underneath? Ben Flood's head lay where Smitho thought his shoulder should be. It was all wrong. His face was grey and dark clotted blood sat between his lips and crept onto his clean shaved skin. His eyes stared vacantly towards the heavens, black and dull and dry. Flies crept in and out of his nose and mouth.

Smitho remained remarkably calm. It was as if he wasn't actually there and was watching a show on the crime channel. He could almost hear a commentary going on in his head..."The victim had died instantly... his chest wounds were not conducive to survival..." He stared at Ben Flood. The flies formed a dark buzzing cloud around them both. He stared and wondered how someone could look so different in death. This once man-mountain looked like a small grotesquely broken puppet. His life-force – his spirit had gone, abandoned him, and only a collapsed empty shell was left.

Without thinking Smitho let go of the corner of the black sheet and the breeze blew it open against the side of the police truck. As he drew his eyes away from Ben Flood's unrecognisable face, he looked at the bloodied sheet as it stuck to the vehicle. The jet black sheet was decorated with occasional thin white lines and curves. It was familiar... But from where? He stared at it as if in a trance. He'd seen it several times over the last few months he was sure... But where?

As the realisation slowly dawned he recoiled from his spot next to the mangled corpse. As he rose and spun away, he immediately crashed down onto the blood soaked bitumen as his head spun and his brain screamed... This could not be happening...

The dead policeman had been wrapped in an ISIS flag.

Chapter 23

Smitho lay flat on the warm, sticky bitumen. His knees, his hands and the left side of his head all hurt form hitting the road hard. He knew he had small shards of gravel stuck in the palms of both hands. He tried to clear his head which had become immersed in a dull fog. He tried to rationalise. He couldn't be safe here. He had to get away. Ben Flood had been blown to pieces here. Surely Mick was dead too. The smoke... The explosion... ISIS must have come after Mick. The stupid prick had dared them to. What a fucking arsehole. Ben Flood... Poor Ben... Wrong place, wrong time poor bastard. He had to get away from here but first he had to alert the authorities of the severity of the drama which was unfolding. Other lives were likely at risk. These murdering pricks were likely still at large.

Smitho slowly peeled himself off the tarmac and stood up. He absently picked the gravel from the palms of his hands. He then turned towards the police vehicle again and he pulled his iPhone from his pocket. He hit the entry code and selected the camera function. He moved in close to the truck and took the best part of twenty photos of the macabre scene. Ben Flood, the flag, the shattered vehicles. He then switched to video mode and walked around both vehicles taking 5-10 second video clips from every angle. When satisfied he had captured every detail he pocketed his phone and turned away. His conscience told him to turn back and cover Ben Flood again to give him some dignity. But there was no dignity to be gained here - at all. The best thing Smitho could do now was to alert the rest of the community to the nightmare which had occurred here. He was unwavering. He did not turn back. He walked slowly and carefully back across the Rankin Bridge to his waiting tow-truck.

His thoughts were in turmoil. This atrocity had happened on Australian soil. This was not North Africa or the Middle East. This was Stewarts River, New South Wales, Australia. This was a country where everyone – all races – people from all over the planet - lived together and thrived together. This was a screaming insult to a whole nation. In Smitho's mind this was a declaration of war. Smitho was a pacifist. He hated bloodshed. He hated war. He had two uncles who had been killed in Vietnam. His grandfather had been a Rat of Tobruk and had suffered mentally for 60 years afterwards. He had attended the funeral of a close school friend's son who had been killed in Afghanistan two years earlier. Smitho detested violence… But these murdering motherfuckers had to be blown to fuck once and for all… And he was now about to do his bit for the war against terrorism. It was his duty. He was now in the service of his country.

When he reached the tow-truck he climbed back into the cab. He slumped in the worn driver's seat and stare back across the bridge. The broken vehicles and the broken body sat under the heavy black sky. Smitho did not understand how this day had changed so dramatically. Suddenly he felt nauseous. He realised his arms and legs were shaking uncontrollably.

"Fuck," he gasped. "Fucking fuck…"

He fumbled in his pocket for his iPhone. He held it in both hands but found it difficult to hit the correct numbers for his entry code. After several attempts he was eventually in. He scrolled through his contact list. Dean Brody, the copper on the radio this morning, was in his contact list somewhere. He'd played golf with him several times and had consumed a few shandies afterwards. Once again his shaking thumbs found it difficult to touch the correct parts of the screen. He cancelled several calls to other friends close in the contact list who he tried to phone by mistake, then suddenly Dean Brody's name and mobile number filled the screen. He hit the call button.

Smitho sat in his cab and willed Dean to answer. The phone rang and rang. "Answer the bloody phone Deano… For fuck sake…" When the call diverted to message bank Smitho hung up and called again. He repeated this exercise four times before Dean Brody finally answered. He barked down the phone, "Hi Smitho – I'm a bit busy right at the minute – can I call you back."

Smitho almost screamed down the phone, "I'm at the Rankin Bridge – Ben Flood is dead... Ben Flood is dead..."

Dean Brody forgot whatever else he was busy with.

"Whoa slow down Smitho, slow down..."

"I can't slow down he's fucking dead – been shot in the chest – absolutely blown to bits..."

"Smitho... Just listen... Take a deep breath and then tell me slowly what is going on."

"For fuck sake Dean just fucking listen – Ben Flood is dead. I'm going to send you some pictures..."

As Dean Brody talked into his phone he realised that Smitho had hung up. "Stupid Prick," he hissed. He hit the redial button. After several seconds he could hear Smitho's phone ringing but it went straight to message bank. "Thank you for calling Smiths Car Maintenance and Towing. I'm out on a job at the minute. Please leave your name and number and I'll call back as soon as I can. Please drive carefully and have a great day..."

At the message tone Dean Brody barked – "Smitho...Phone me back NOW."

As he hit the hang-up logo a small bird chirped announcing that he'd received a text message. It was from Smitho. He opened the message. There was no text – just a logo stating that he'd received a photo. He tapped the logo on the screen and waited for the photo to appear. For the hundredth time he cursed and wished he'd traded this old banger of a phone for an iPhone. This was way too bloody slow. After 30 painful seconds the screen of his phone filled with vibrant colour. He stared at the screen. His brain had stopped. He did not want to comprehend what he was looking at.

In the palm of his hand, the dead eyes of Ben Flood stared vacantly from a grey face. Bloody froth and purple blood clot dribbled from his lips and nose. His police shirt was purple with blood and in the lower half of the picture a massive ragged wound exposed shattered ribs and obliterated muscle and lung tissue.

He stared for only a couple of seconds but time had stopped...the seconds took an age to pass. Ben Flood. Dead. He was here this morning. He'd talked to him thirty minutes ago. He was larger than life... An unstoppable Arnold Schwarzenegger look alike. Vibrant. Loud. What the hell... This was no photo shopped image. This was so real. Fuck. You couldn't fake dead like this. This was gross and very, very real. He had to move. He had to relay this information to all the boys out and about immediately. He had to get his superiors in the loop ASAP. They were going to need help.

Just as the hideous spell was broken and he reached for the radio microphone, the little bird inside his phone chirped again. Another text message from Smitho. This time no text but a video icon appeared. He hit the icon and stared at the screen. It was going to take for ever. Bloody phone. Why had he never got himself an iPhone? Even his kids had iPhones... As he waited he lifted the radio microphone to his lips and depressed the talk button.

"Calling all cars, calling all cars... This is Stewarts River Dispatch... Stand by for emergency call, repeat stand by for emergency call..."

When the video start logo appeared on his ancient mobile phone he hit the start button with his thumb and stared at the screen. Constable Leonie Johnston, recently arrived from Melbourne University with a degree in Forensic Entomology and Senior Sergeant Lou Tattis, over weight, aged sixty and longing for retirement, both emerged from their own workstations within the building. They had heard Dean's radio message via their own personal radios. They piled swiftly into the radio room through the open door and stared over Dean's shoulders as the video began to play.

Mick Gallagher's shot up ute filled the screen and Smitho's voice croaked, "That's Mick the vet's old truck – it's been shot up badly but there's no sign of Mick anywhere...poor bastard's probably dead – there's blood on his driver's seat..." The camera then scanned around to the police four wheel drive, complete with blood spattered windscreen.

Smitho walked closer and slowly the video screen was filled with the mangled remains of Ben Flood – flies and all. Senior Sergeant Lou Tattis turned abruptly away from the hideous vision and vomited noisily on the office floor while grasping onto the dispatch desk to stop himself from collapsing. The young police woman gasped and gripped suddenly onto Dean Brody's upper arm.

The camera now moved from the lifeless policeman to a black sheet covered in blood clots and white lines which stretched from under his body and spread across the road beside him with some of the top edge stuck to the vehicle.

Nobody had to tell Dean Brody or Constable Johnston what they were looking at.

Smitho's voice simply stated, "It's ISIS...They've come to kill Mick..."

Chapter 24

Dean Brody barked into the police radio microphone, "Calling all cars... Calling all cars... This is Stewarts River Dispatch. Please change to frequency code 147 and await instructions..." On this radio coded frequency only the police could receive and reply to messages.

As he waited a few seconds for the cars to change wavelengths he sent Smitho's photo and video by e-mail to his work computer. He sat at his desk and put on his headset, which comprised of earphones and an attached microphone, thus freeing up his hands to use the computer keyboard.

On Frequency Code 147 he spoke clearly and with firm authority.

"Calling all cars... We have an emergency situation at Rankin Bridge, two kilometres south of Stewarts River on Stewarts Road. Potentially armed gunmen at large. Explosions and shooting reported at 4016 Stewarts Road two kilometres further south. Premises is local Veterinary Surgery. One police fatality at Rankin Bridge. Status of occupants at 4016 unknown. Please approach with extreme caution and leave radio lines open at all times. Be aware this situation is potentially a terrorist attack..."

While talking on air Dean had lined up a conference call to the police hierarchy in Stewarts River, Tamworth, Sydney, Brisbane and the Australian Capital Territory (ACT). As he signed off to the squad cars he hit the call request icon on his computer and within 30 seconds was explaining to multiple senior officers the state of play as he understood it so far. Once he had briefed them of the details he announced that he was e-mailing a picture and video from the scene directly to them all.

Two minutes later Police Captain Peter Green was bolting through the clubhouse at Stewarts River Golf Club on his way to take immediate command at Stewarts River Police Station.

Six minutes later Police Captain Roy Podolski of Tamworth was briefing staff to drive the one and a half hours straight to Stewarts River to provide immediate back-up to the local police involved in the incident.

Within seven minutes Police Commissioners from Sydney, Brisbane and the ACT were briefing government anti-terrorism departments on the situation evolving in western New South Wales. Anti-terrorism personnel would be flown to Stewarts River immediately.

Within 15 minutes the anti-terrorism agencies had flagged the potential terrorist attack to anti-terrorism agencies around the world.

Forty-five minutes after Dean Brody had passed the photo and video on to his superiors in Australia they had been shared by government agencies in the US, the UK, France, Germany, Italy, India, Pakistan and Indonesia. The acting Australian Prime Minister, Barnaby Joyce, was briefed while visiting a beef farm in Northern Queensland. The actual Australian Prime Minister Malcom Turnbull was briefed shortly afterwards as he flew thirty-thousand feet above the Red Sea in an RAAF Hercules Aircraft, en route to a surprise visit with Australian troops in Afghanistan to raise morale.

An hour and ten minutes after Smitho took his gruesome images the effects were reverberating around the globe. In California, while enjoying a quiet round of golf with the Chinese ambassador to the United States and his entourage, United States President Donald Trump was alerted to the fatal attack in Australia by his security advisors.

While having a quiet nightcap with Camilla Parker Bowles after a birthday party at Buckingham Palace for one of Prince Charles' favourite god children, the British Prime Minister, Theresa May, was briefed on the terror attack in New South Wales by agents from MI6.

After his call to the police Smitho had decided to block the road with his truck and to only allow police or armed forces access to the bridge. He had manoeuvred the huge truck so that it now blocked both lanes on and off the bridge on the north side.

He could see no activity towards town or on the other side of the bridge. He sat and waited. He hadn't heard from Dean Brody. Fuck. Should he call again? Fuck.

There were several small townships between here and Albeston on the road south. There was likely to be traffic heading to Stewarts River this morning from the south. He had to divert people. He had to avert them from entering what he now deemed a "crime scene"… or more likely a "war zone".

As he sat and stared over the bridge and down the road to the south Smitho had an epiphany. Facebook… He could message people on Facebook. He had quite a few relatives and clients on the south side of the bridge. He could warn people and summon help by messaging on Facebook. He was excited at the thought. His kids would be proud of him. They were always telling him that most people spent half their waking hours looking at Facebook.

He stared at his mobile phone and tried to remember how to send messages. He hit the Facebook icon and he was straight in. He needed people to know that this was deadly serious and not a hoax in any way. He scanned through the photos he had taken and then the video clips. He highlighted the ones which he thought would be least disturbing to any viewer, but which would give his message a sense of emergency and reality. He reassessed them once he'd selected the images. They were all vile. Maybe he should message people and hope they took him seriously without the horrific images. Shit… What a predicament… No fuck it… He couldn't send any of these. They were just too grotesque. He quickly searched his friends to the south of the bridge, He could message Paul Yule, the diesel mechanic at Brinbudden, 15 kilometres away. His shop-front was right on the main road. He occasionally did NRMA work. He might even have signage to put up on the road. He could also message Peter Lilley and John Rosenbaum. Both were graziers whose properties sat on either side of Stewarts Road. They were mature and sensible. Peter Lilley was a Vietnam War veteran. He highlighted all three names and then wrote the message.

"Emergency between Stewarts River Veterinary Hospital and Rankin Bridge. Avoid Stewarts Road at all costs." As an afterthought he wrote, "Massive Chemical Spill". He thought to himself that a scenario involving dangerous chemicals would deter people. Nobody wanted to inhale chemical fumes. He then added, "Please stop vehicles form heading north past your properties."

Smitho thought his wording was good. He thought the chemical spill story would avoid melodrama and that the normal general public would not want to come anywhere near the area. Chemical spills had actually occurred out here in the sticks a couple of times in the last decade. People knew how serious they could be. He read it again and hit the post button.

"Hopefully Pete and John will block the road with farm vehicles," Smitho said quietly to himself as he stared at the screen on his mobile phone. He noticed that he only had one bar of battery left and it was flashing. Bugger. He put the phone back in his pocket and stared back across the bridge.

Smitho was never the best with technology. He had not messaged Paul Yule, Peter Lilley and John Rosenbaum. He had actually sent a post to all of his three hundred and twenty-three friends – not only in and around Stewarts River, but also to friends in Queensland, Western Australia, New Zealand and Canada too. Not only would they receive a message about a chemical spill on Stewarts Road, they would receive 5 photos of smashed vehicles and a dead police officer lying on an ISIS flag. The two videos sent would give some recipients nightmares for years to come.

Within minutes the horrific photos and videos had been viewed and shared, and viewed and shared, around the entire planet. Cyberspace took the pictures and video to all states in Australia, New Zealand and Canada and then on to 200 more countries around the world. Facebook was abhorred and took the graphic images down very quickly. Smitho's Facebook page was frozen within twenty-three minutes of his post. But... The damage was done. Over two and a half million views... Smitho had gone viral. The man himself was none the wiser. He sat in his monstrous tow truck and stared across the Rankin Bridge, his phone dead in his pocket.

Donald Trump learned the details of Ben Flood's death on his "Twitter" account 17 minutes before he learned the news from his security team. The images rattled him enough that he four-putted on the Par 3 fifteenth.

Chapter 25

When Mick woke he was in a small private room at the hospital. He lay on a bed which bent in the middle and raised the top half of his body above the level of his feet. He was lying but almost sitting at the same time. There was a drip line taped into his right forearm attached to a large bag of fluid on a drip stand with a machine counting the drops being pumped into him. A clip was attached to his right index finger, connected to a machine monitoring his oxygen saturation, heart rate and rhythm. The ECG line on the same machine lit up repeatedly with a nice consistent steady trace. His chest felt tightly dressed and he was aware of large diameter, plastic tubes exiting from the bed clothes and carrying cloudy red fluid to somewhere under the bed. His head was swathed in bandages. He was uncomfortably aware that there was a piece of plastic tubing extending up his old fella... WTF?

His left hand was held tightly by a beautiful, blonde, tired looking nurse sitting by his bed. They both looked at each other. His ex-wife was still a stunning woman - tiny, slim, steel blue eyes, smooth blemish free skin. Just gorgeous.

They both knew they still loved each other... Just couldn't live with each other.

Mick the philandering bastard knew it was all his fault. Too many extramarital shaggings... again... and again... He just couldn't stop.

She leaned over and kissed him.

Pain racked his head and chest as he tried to move towards her.

"Don't move Mick. You're a mess."

For some reason Mick's brain played a video of a plumber's truck driving along a country road. He couldn't understand why. There was a vague uneasiness which came as the truck drove away. Where on earth did that come from?

Tears slid down Fiona's cheeks as she looked at him for several long seconds. She shook her head and slowly continued.

"You presented this morning with grossly contaminated pneumothorax, with a collapsed lung and five broken ribs. You've got chest drains in, and your chest wall has been closed and pulled back together. A piece of concrete from the Rankin Bridge was removed from a hole in the top of your head – where there's a nice hairline fracture of your skull. You've received four litres of blood and more antibiotics and painkillers than you can poke a stick at. You have a urinary catheter in until you're allowed to move… You were in surgery for 4 hours. You arrested twice."

She paused. He was looking at her in disbelief. He was finding it hard to take in what he was hearing. Her voice cracked as she went on.

"It's a helluva way to get to come and see me… You only have to pick up the phone you know…"

Even smiling made Mick's chest ache.

Her face suddenly darkened. Her eyes became cool and hard. She seemed to be staring through him. She said nothing for several long moments. The silence was very pregnant.

"You've really done well this time… Big George is dead. Ben Flood is dead. April's horse is dead. And the Vet Hospital is all but burned to the ground. There are police and army everywhere. Two armed police outside your very door." She turned her head and looked directly towards the door of the small room. There was another long pause before her soft voice carried on.

"The hospital is besieged by TV and radio crews. We can't answer the phones but have to talk to the world's press who want to talk to the man who dared ISIS to kill him and brought the murdering bastards to Western New South Wales to carry out a FATWA. You're world famous now. I'm not allowed to go home. Julia has been moved from uni to a safe house somewhere outside Sydney."

Mick was stunned. His head was having huge problems digesting and making sense of what Fiona was saying.

There was a sharp rap on the door. Another older, plumper nurse that Mick knew as Madelaine Brewer, stuck her head around the door. Madelaine was the owner of Peter the poodle who was in the end stages of congestive heart failure. Mick had spent some long consultations with Madelaine, just lately, discussing Pete's deteriorating condition. Madelaine looked seriously at Fiona and stated, "You might have to come for tea now Fi... Mick's got a visitor."

Fi looked confused.

She repeated, "I think you should come for tea now Fi. Mick's got a visitor." Her words were spoken very deliberately and sounded quite stilted.

Fiona replied, "No it's OK. I'll stay and keep an eye on things. Show them in."

Madelaine looked very red in the face. Sweat beads appeared on her forehead. There was a very long pause.

"It's Doctor Chowdry's wife..."

The colour drained from Fiona's face.

"I'll be there in a minute."

She looked straight at Mick, her eyes now very cool.

"She's your best friend's wife you stupid bastard. Why do you have to ruin life for everyone around you?" Her eyes were now filled with tears threatening to escape.

As she rose, Beatrice Chowdry swept into the room. Both women froze and stared at each other for interminable seconds. You could have cut the air with a knife.

Then Fi turned her head towards Mick and stated, "I'll be back later. You need someone capable to look after you."

She turned and was gone in a microsecond.

Chapter 26

Beatrice beamed at Mick. She was totally unmoved by Fiona's parting comments. She was wearing a beautiful floral dress with a plunging neckline. Her ebony hair shone as if she wore a halo. Her make-up was from a fashion shoot on Vogue - ruby red, moist, shining lips and long, thick black eyelashes around animated, twinkling brown eyes. Her skin was like porcelain – glowing and unblemished. My God she was just beautiful.

"Such great news. You've done amazingly well to survive the day and they're going to transfer you to Sydney in the next couple of days when you're more stable. A couple of weeks there – probably The Royal North Shore – and then home for rehab. I'm going to prepare the spare room."

She paused, her eyes twinkling.

"Well actually if you need intensive rehab I might move you into my room for extra special care."

She grinned and bent and kissed his cheek and lingered long enough for Mick to once again stare at the Promised Land. Beautiful... Just beautiful... The porcelain skin extended from her face deep into her soft bountiful cleavage. My God...

Mick felt a familiar tingling in his groin but the tingling abated when the stirring caused the plastic catheter to kink in his urethra. That felt all sorts of wrong. Especially when he knew the catheter extended to a litre capacity bag of urine hanging somewhere under his bed.

Beatrice continued.

"Now they've told me I can only visit for a couple of minutes as you need to get as much rest as possible. So I'm just going to love you and leave you and I'll be back first thing in the morning. I'll keep you posted on what's on the news. You've been on all the channels including BBC world and Al Jazeera. You're being held up as an anti-ISIS hero. You're just magnificent..."

She wrapped her arms gently around his neck and cuddled in close. Her luscious fruity smell and the cosy softness of her plentiful bosom against his chest made him feel elated. Maybe the drugs helped too.

After a couple of minutes she rose with tears in her eyes and kissed him on the lips. They looked into one another's eyes.

"It's all going to have a wonderfully happy ending." She whispered.

She kissed him on the lips again then departed without another word, waving and blowing a kiss as she passed through the door.

Mick stared at the door. He thought she was a goddess. The perfect woman. This was what he'd been waiting for all his life. Recuperation at Beatrice's place. He could handle that. He replayed the vision of her delicious cleavage in his head again and again...

Once again the discomfort of the catheter dampened his spirits.

Chapter 27

Mick slept fitfully. Pictures of Beatrice's wrangler clad arse and perfectly formed breasts brightened his dreams. But pictures of Big George's exploding head and Ben Flood blown all over his police truck tormented him. Worst was when his dad appeared, headless but screaming. Mick couldn't get away. His dad was there in front of him screaming for help. Nobody came. A huge black horse screamed and whinnied and reared up all over him, battering his chest and his head with it's huge leaden feet. The pain was horrific. He was frantically trying to stitch the horse's head in place. The head was attached to the body by threads of shredded muscle and skin and there was blood flying everywhere - up Mick's nose and into his mouth. He could not breathe. He was suffocating. The blood was stinging his eyes. He could barely see a thing. But he could not stop. He had to make the horse whole again. It was Julia's horse... She was here somewhere but he could not see her. She was screaming. "Don't let my horse die you arsehole... You've fucked up everything else in my life..." Around and around the screaming, the mangled bodies, the pain and the suffocation... Each episode of the dream slid into the next - again and again.

He slept and dreamed for minutes at a time. He stared at the walls for what seemed like endless hours. He was too scared to sleep. The clock on the wall was broken – it wouldn't move. The same second ticked over and over again for hours. Was he alive? Or was he dead? Or was he somewhere in between?

Faceless nurses came and went. He wasn't sure if they were in his dreams or they were actually there. No faces, no form. Vague shapes. Ghosts.

His machinery beeped and whirred – like Japanese water torture – the machinery noises repeated and repeated and repeated - and time stood still.

Fluid moved through tubes into his body and through tubes out of his body. He could feel every tiny drop entering and leaving.

He was aware of commotion. People running in and out. Flashing lights. Red and blue. The ceiling was flashing. Red and blue. Sirens. Wailing sirens. Grey people talking above him. Dreams? Reality? Which was which? It was all the same.

Pain waxed and waned. His whole body was a dull throb of pain. His head had different pains from minute to minute. His whole head, the top of his head, the deep parts of his head. Acute screaming, electrical pain. Deep, low throbbing pain. He had sharp, shrieking pain behind his eyes. He had dull niggling pain on top of his head. Bizarre ringing in his ears came and went.

God he was tired.

Breathing was tiring. In - Out - In – Out. Each inspiration and each expiration brought it's own wearing, aching pain.

He couldn't move. If he moved in any microscopic way his head would erupt in even more pain. He had to lie still.

He was being tortured. The nurses were keeping him alive so he could feel more pain. They were managing it all. They were torturing him because he was such a prick.

Fuck!

Fuck!

Fuck!

Chapter 28

The ceiling lights in the room were off but the illumination from the life sustaining machinery around Mick's bed and the small wall lamp above the oxygen line going into the wall a few feet away lit the bed and the centre of the room well. In the grey periphery of the room Mick saw the door opening. A figure shuffled through the door. It closed again quietly.

The figure of Dr Rashid Chowdry, tired and moving awkwardly under a large rucksack moved slowly to the end of the bed. Mick thought that he was dreaming again. He had to be. Chowdry was overseas visiting the rellies and fattening up on mum's curry puffs. The apparition stayed however. The unmistakeable face of Rashid Chowdry was staring calmly at him from the end of his sick-bed. Was this real? Or was Mick still away with the fairies? Slowly a smile spread across Chowdry's face and laugh lines cracked around his eyes.

"I hear you've had a twat of a day my big Aussie mate." Chowdry was now grinning widely.

Mick's face lit up. It was absolutely wonderful to see his best friend of 20 years. He beamed through his pain. Chowdry wrestled the rucksack from his back and deposited it with a thud on the floor at the end of the bed. He looked absolutely knackered.

Mick's words crept out quietly – "I thought you were in India."

"Just back tonight." The familiar voice had a marked Indian accent and sounded exhausted. It always amused Mick that his friend sounded more Indian than ever after a visit to his rellies in New Delhi.

Chowdry moved up the side of the bed and bent over and gently hugged his friend.

"What on earth have you been up to?" the doctor asked, looking into Mick's eyes.

"Had a shit of a day mate. Looks like these ISIS bastards came after me. All to do with me going off at the pricks on YouTube all those months ago after dad died. You'd think they'd have bigger fish to fry."

Chowdry looked steadily into Mick's eyes. "You did actually asked them to come and have a crack at you, you dickhead. You challenged them in front of the whole fucking world."

Mick knew it was true. He just couldn't believe that it had actually happened.

"They killed Julia's horse. Chopped it's fucking head off. Just like they did to my old man. Not exactly a subtle calling card. How the fuck do you cut a fucking horse's head off? A moving fucking target. It should have kicked the shit out of them. "

Chowdry still looking into his eyes suggested – "Probably put Xylazine in his drip."

Mick was confused. He hadn't thought of that. He lay contemplating... How would they know how to do that? Clever bastards. Clever, evil, devious bastards.

Chowdry was up on his feet. He'd pulled on a pair of latex examination gloves from a box on top of one of the machines that buzzed and produced an ECG image. He was studying Mick's charts. He moved back to the side of the bed and examined his colour, listened to his chest very carefully with the stethoscope left hanging on the drip stand and then, checked the drains and the drain bottles. He then checked the IV line in Mick's arm, the drip machine and checked his watch.

In a quiet voice he asked Mick, "Are you sore?"

"My oath", Mick whispered.

"The timing is good. We can safely top up your pain meds now."

He picked a small vial from the array of drugs in a cabinet below one of the whirring machines. He flicked the top off the vial and drew several cc of clear fluid out into a small syringe with a fine needle attached. He then turned back to the drip machine and picked up a portion of drip tubing containing a small rubber injection port. He wiped a metho swab over the rubber end of the port and slowly and carefully injected the syringe contents into the drip line. He then punched a few illuminated pads on the drip machine itself and the machine started pumping fluid faster than in the minutes before. Mick was delighted his friend knew exactly what he was doing.

"You should feel better in a minute or two."

Within a few seconds the pain subsided dramatically. Mick relaxed. He watched his friend as he placed the used needle carefully in a sharps bin and the empty syringe into the general waste bin on the floor. Slowly however Mick began to feel tired. He also began to feel light-headed and weak. He couldn't feel his arms. When he talked he slurred.

"Musst be good sshit…"

"Only the best my friend. I'm pretty good when it comes to putting things in drips."

The sentence lingered and Mick's thoughts spun as he tried to make sense of what he'd just been told. His mate was taking the piss.

Chowdry dragged the rucksack around to the side of the bed. He lowered his face to Mick's and looked intently into his eyes. Staring – unblinking – saying nothing.

Mick could not move. He could only groan when he tried to talk.

Chowdry's eyes were focused somewhere inside Mick's head. The stare was cold and unwavering. Mick's guts slowly knotted.

Chowdry bent and fumbled with the top of the rucksack. He pulled the top open and reached inside with both arms. His eyes once again returned to Mick. He stared right into Mick's very core. The stare was ice cold. Mick felt his sole freezing. Fear gripped his helpless body.

Suddenly Chowdrey rose to his full height and grunted maniacally as he heaved a large black dripping mass from inside the rucksack. As he raised it high above the bed Mick's brain began to scream. The realisation was excruciating. He was staring at the severed head of Julia's dead horse. The huge, blank, blind eyes looked demonic. Slimy red froth spewed from both lips and nostrils, and dripping, dark red, stringy blood clots hung from butchered neck muscles. Chowdry held it high above the bed for only a brief second and then dropped it directly on top of the bed.

Air exploded out of Mick's lungs as the weight of the huge, black severed head sank into his compromised chest. His brain was imploding. What the fuck? What the fuck? This was not happening. This could not be happening. The bloody, black mass lay on top of him - suffocating him - stealing his precious oxygen. It was huge and black and soaked in it's own blood. The grotesque mass of horse flesh stared at Mick with unseeing eyes. What the fuck?

Chowdry stood and stared at Mick. He was absolutely delighted to see this man suddenly shitting himself, not in control and terrified. He stood and watched and exulted in the moment. He was enjoying his triumph immensely. He really wanted to make this prick suffer. This malignant bastard who had pretended to be his best friend. He had dreamt of this moment. He had begged God for this moment, and now he wanted it to last. For both of them. He needed to savour it as much as he needed Mick to suffer. He wanted him to feel pain and anguish. He wanted him to be tortured. He wanted him to feel helpless. He wanted him to know that he'd brought this on himself - the spineless, amoral bastard. He paced from once side of the bed to the other. Watching. Gloating.

Mick felt nauseous. The room was spinning. Realisation was painful. Realisation was appalling. His realisation was beyond belief. This was retribution. This was not ISIS. This was very, very personal revenge.

Chowdry bent and heaved the dead horse's head onto the floor. It thudded loudly as it hit the tiles. It bounced bizarrely and then slid several inches. It came to rest at the end of bloody skid marks and then slowly oozed red, black, frothy mucous from every gaping orifice. It looked grotesque and ridiculously surreal lying on the polished floor of the immaculately clean hospital room.

Chowdry's face was once again in front of Mick, staring at him intently – cold and poisonous.

"Penny dropped yet?" he hissed. His eyes burned into Mick's for several long moments before he continued.

"You've been shagging Beatrice - you blind, heartless bastard. I hope you fucking enjoyed it because she was your last shag on this earth. You're about to join your old man."

"I know there were others before you, but they were fleeting encounters... enough to keep her happy." He slid one hand onto Mick's pillow and grabbed a handful of bandages on top of his head and pulled his face even closer. The pain in Mick's head reached a crescendo and he could smell Chowdry's breath and feel the spit from his lips on his face as he continued his rant.

"But with you... She's fallen in love with you, you bastard. You've been shagging everybody else in town for years. Why couldn't you leave her alone? She was the one thing in my life that mattered. I left to teach her a lesson, to let her know how she couldn't survive here without me, and then you decide to move into the gap."

"You bastard. You sat and listened to me pour my heart out that I was losing her. I told you my every thought and feeling about her. You gave me advice. You told me to give her space, and I did. And you started shagging her two weeks later. Two fucking weeks later."

Tears had welled in Chowdry's eyes. They slowly dripped down his face and onto the bed sheets.

"And now she doesn't want to know me. I'm finished. Gone. She's in love with you – you bastard. Why can't she see that you'd shag your own sister if you had the chance? You're a dirty fucking male slut. She thinks you're a God. She thinks you can right every wrong on the planet. She thinks you're her knight in shining armour. For you, she's just another root. You're best friend's wife. You are a pathetic human being. You are fucking disgusting."

"You think you're such a hero for ranting at ISIS. You're nothing. Why would they waste their time coming after you? You're just a mouthpiece with middle age hormone problems. You are just scum."

"She tells me she loves you."

"She tells me you make her whole again."

Chowdry let go of Mick's head but kept staring into his eyes. He stooped and reached into the rucksack. With a leering grin spreading across his face he stood and pulled his wife's severed head out of the rucksack. He broke into wild, hysterical laughter as he saw the sheer terror and disbelief in Mick's eyes. He lifted Beatrice's blood covered head high above the bed and looked from Mick's face to hers, and back again, delighting in the incredible power of the moment. Then suddenly he dropped his wife's head directly on to Mick's chest.

"Well she's not whole anymore."

The world was moving in slow motion for Mick. He tried to scream. He tried to tear himself out of the bed. Nothing would work. He was paralysed. He could make no noise – move no muscle. He tasted and smelled vomitus in his throat and began choking.

The blood covered head of Beatrice had a grimacing vacant stare as it bounced off the bed and skidded across the floor leaving a trail of red-black blood behind it. It came to rest against the wall wrapped in blood matted hair with mutilated bone, muscle and cartilage extending grotesquely from the once beautiful neck.

Chapter 29

Chowdry had a scalpel in his hand. He leaned in to stare in Mick's face again. His bloodshot eyes and grimacing features bore no resemblance to any sane person. Something in his brain had broken, his psyche had unravelled.

"You're about to be reunited with your father." Chowdry seemed to take great pleasure in his revelation. He was laughing quietly as he spoke. "Rather poetic that you both die in the same way, don't you think. You both spent time in places you should never have gone. Neither of you ever thought of the possible consequences. Both so short sighted and ego driven."

"And don't worry. They won't pin your death on me. The benefit of powdered latex examination gloves – no fingerprints. Good - huh? I'm sure the world will blame ISIS. I wrapped the dead cop in an ISIS flag. It's amazing what you can get through customs these days. Cost me four dollars in a market in New Delhi. The icing on the cake that one. ISIS can take the credit for everything. They will probably claim responsibility anyway. They seem to claim responsibility for everything else." He laughed to himself. "According to immigration and passport control I'm still in India. I came in on a false passport. Very easily obtained in a poor country like India. Our IT is better than anywhere else in the world and the product, my new passport, is absolutely first class. Four hundred bucks. Cheap as chips. Absolutely stunning."

"I'll be back in New Delhi tomorrow night. Maybe even before the news of your deaths breaks there. I'm currently on a trek in the foothills of the Himalayas in Uttarakhand. The authorities may take a few days to find me. I'll come back in shock for the funeral of my poor butchered wife and my best friend. I will mourn you both very sombrely. I will be devastated. I will condemn terrorism but I will not challenge ISIS to come and take me on. I want a quiet life."

"I'm about to remove your head you arsehole. I'm going to do it slowly so you can appreciate my surgical skill."

He gently pressed the scalpel blade in the groove in the right side of Mick's neck. Mick could feel the pressure of the blade but could not react in any way at all.

"First I'm cutting your jugular vein."

As Chowdry said this Mick felt a sharp stab then heard a swooshing noise as shining dark red blood ran out onto Chowdry's hand and cascaded on to the bed linen. Chowdry continued to stare into Mick's eyes. Mick was becoming extremely tired."

After several seconds Chowdry continued, "Not long left now. I might take out your carotid artery - but then you'd be gone too fast. I think I'll just sit here and watch you go slowly and then drop your head over there with the bitch."

Mick was screaming inside his head. As he watched his lifeblood spread across the crumpled hospital sheet, and listened as it fizzed and spurted from the wound in his throat, he felt duller and duller. He fought hard to remain conscious. Darkness was calling. The lights on the machines were fading. Chowdry's, now blood spattered face, floated in and out of focus in front of him. He could see his tormentor's leering grin. He couldn't move. He couldn't scream. He was dying helplessly... No! No! This cannot be how it ends.

Julia was telling him it was OK to go. Her face replaced Chowdry's. She was comforting him. "It's OK dad. It's OK. Don't worry." He saw her being born. Her beautiful radiant mother presenting her to him wrapped in a bunny rug. Both his mother and father were enjoying their new grand-daughter laughing and smiling. They both looked young and fit. He was graduating as a vet after years and years of studying. Robes and all. He was playing with Gwen his childhood golden retriever his first love...

Chapter 30

Chowdry suddenly lurched forward, smacking his head straight into Mick's face. The sudden blow pulled Mick back to the here and now. In the same instant Mick was aware of a distant cracking noise. Chowdry fell onto the bed, further crushing Mick's chest. Mick desperately gasped for air as Chowdrey slowly slid off the side of the bed and crumpled to a flaccid heap on the floor. Mick did not understand. His ex-wife stood beside the bed screaming like a banshee and holding on to a blood stained fire extinguisher. A young man in a white coat with thick bottle top black glasses pushed passed her and immediately reached for the right side of his neck. He pushed his fingers deep into the tissues around the haemorrhaging wound. He looked as green as Mick looked white. Despite his colour, the young doctor's brain was in over drive and he pulled up handfuls of bed linen and pushed them forcefully into the wound in the groove on Mick's neck. He had to stop the bleeding. He had to stop the bleeding, or this was a dead man. The young man was suddenly shouting at the top of his lungs.

"Hello - Emergency – Emergency - Critical Patient – Need Crash-Cart, Surgical kit and prep and O positive blood immediately. All hands on deck immediately! Immediately!"

Fiona still was screaming insanely at the top of her voice.

Mick's brain was screaming at the man with the glasses, "Keep the pressure on. For god's sake keep the pressure on. Just don't let go."

Fiona was screaming at Mick, screaming for help, screaming at God. And while she screamed she dropped the fire extinguisher and grabbed Mick's limp right hand and squeezed it for all she was worth.

"Stay with me Mick. Stay with me," she screamed. She stood behind the intense young doctor who was focused once again on the same dying man he had valiantly helped save several hours earlier. She stared into Mick's fading eyes and willed him to fight.

The flaccid form of Chowdry was forgotten under their feet. He did not move at all. He lay on the floor barely breathing, his face flattened onto the tiles of the floor which were awash in Mick's blood, mingled with the blood of a murdered woman and the blood of a butchered horse. The horses severed head lay grotesquely on the floor behind Chowdry. His wife's head lay against the wall several feet behind the horse's head. Beatrice was unrecognisable. The skin of her face was blue-grey. Thin black lips were pulled back in a hideous, silent scream. Dull, unseeing eyes stared vacantly. The once lustrous and vibrant black hair was now dull and plastered to her face. Every part of the head was covered in dark red purple blood.

Mick tried to focus on Fiona but she was swimming in and out of focus. He vaguely heard more voices screaming. Nurses and policemen were now flooding into the room.

Dr Glasses was barking instructions.

Fuck he was tired. Very tired.

He slowly succumbed to the darkness.

Chapter 31

Mick slowly became aware of bright lights and ticking, whirring electronic devices around him. His head throbbed. His eyes ached. He felt dull pain in the right side of his neck. The pain in his chest was excruciating. He lay for minutes eyes closed - focusing on the pain, the noises - trying to make sense of it all.

Slowly he realised someone was holding his hand – squeezing gently.

When he opened his eyes the world swam before him. It took several minutes for the blurred hospital room to come into focus. His beautiful wife - ex-wife – Fiona was sitting in the chair by his bed squeezing his hand. She looked pale and tired with deep, dark rings around her eyes.

They looked at each other for several long minutes before she spoke.

"It's good to see you Mick." She sounded absolutely knackered.

"You're a stubborn shit. You died twice again last night… Two cardiac arrests… Came back from both." She paused.

"You didn't have a lot of blood left when I came in and smashed Chowdry with the fire extinguisher. Young Dr Kirkton was the hero – he dived in and closed both severed ends of your jugular vein with his fingers and the bed sheets for almost 15 minutes before Martin Price arrived and ligated them both. You arrested just after Martin finished the ligatures and again 25 minutes after that. Paddles, adrenaline, cardiac massage, IPPV and you came back both times. The second time you were gone for eight and a half minutes. You took 6 litres of blood over the last 4 hours. You're a tough bastard. When you're strong enough they're going to fly you to Sydney to reconnect the ends of your jugular vein. You'll be as good as new."

Tears were trickling steadily down her cheeks

"I was terrified. I thought you were dead."

She paused again and wiped away tears with the back of her hand.

"But you're going to be fine - you bloody, fucking, arsehole, prick."

She choked and coughed and spluttered as she continued to cry and laugh at the same time.

Mick tried to move – tried to talk but the effort shot brutal pain though his chest and neck. She waved a calming hand.

"Don't move. Don't try to talk. You'll be fine."

They stayed in silence for the next couple of minutes. The tears had stopped when she next spoke.

"Beatrice is dead. Chowdry killed her and set fire to the house. The house fire was enough of a distraction for the police to leave you unattended. That's when he made his move and came in here. The police have him in custody."

Mick's brain slowly relived the drama of the night before. The horse's head. The beautiful Beatrice. Her bloodied head lying on the floor staring with dull lifeless eyes. Chowdry. His best mate. Watching him die – slowly – and savouring every moment.

Mick felt nauseated, the pain was excruciating.

He closed his eyes. Darkness threatened to engulf him. He wanted it to engulf him. He wanted to escape. Sleep came and released him from his torture.

He woke. How long later he had no idea. Fiona was still holding his hand. She looked exhausted. She stood.

"I've got to go now and get some sleep. Julia is flying in at three this arvo. I'll bring her straight here. She's distraught. There's a new nurse from Melbourne just started this afternoon – her name is Toni. I'll send her in to do your checks. They're due in about five minutes."

She stood motionless and stared at him for long seconds. Tears again filled her eyes.

"I'll always love you Mick."

She bent, kissed his cheek and was gone.

Chapter 32

Minutes later Mick became aware that someone else was in the room. He opened his eyes to see a gorgeous hourglass figure topped with rolls of shiny dark hair escaping out from under a nurse's hat. He enjoyed the vision. After a couple of minutes checking drip machines and cardiac monitors she turned to look at her patient. Mick beheld an angel. Beautiful olive skin, dark eyes with amazing long black lashes and the most beautiful full red lips he'd ever seen. Her bright grin revealed flawless shining teeth.

"Good morning Mr Mick the Vet. My name is Toni and I'm looking after you today."

As she bent over him to check his dressings Mick got the most wonderful view of his life down the front of her uniform. Flawless olive skin, the most beautiful full bosoms restrained in expensive, ivory, silk lingerie and a stunning large red jewel sitting in her navel. My God she was just the most beautiful thing ever in the history of the universe.

Mick's brain froze. A picture of Beatrice, beautiful and exuberant appeared in his mind's eye. He could smell her and imagined her soft touch on his skin. He could hear her laughing. He could see her mesmerising, hypnotic eyes. He could almost taste her. He could feel her breath on his face. He could see her moist lips as she chuckled and grinned.

Toni the nurse was talking happily away about nothing in particular. He didn't hear a word. His eyes had filled with tears and they were spilling down his cheeks and onto the bed clothes. Suddenly he was sobbing uncontrollably.

Mick knew it was all his fault. Fiona. Julia. Now his best mate. He'd offended him in the worst possible way and turned him into a monster. And Beatrice, the most beautiful Beatrice... What a ridiculous, terrible waste. It was an absolute sin. The woman that he thought might save him from himself was gone - and it was all of his doing. Who was he kidding? Save him from himself. Pig's fucking arse. If Beatrice and he had ever become an item he knew only too well that if another good looking chick looked at him and gave him half a chance he would be off quietly shagging elsewhere in an instant. And without batting an eyelid. He had no conscience at all. He had no morals. The die was cast. He was just a self-centred fucking arsehole. And along the way Big George and Ben Flood. Both dead. Their families distraught and damaged for ever. Fuck. And Judge and Rocky - both dead too. And Zeus, his daughter's pride and joy mutilated and killed horrifically. He was responsible for the complete carnage of the last couple of days. No-one would ever be able to tell him any different. Mick Gallagher was responsible for the most horrific killing spree in the history of Stewarts River. Yet his father was an absolute hero - how could this be so? Why on earth was he, Mick fucking Gallagher, still alive? Why hadn't he been allowed to die? Why had he beaten the odds again and again over the last twenty-four hours? Why had the planets aligned to keep him alive when the others had been killed so horrifically? So that he could be tortured further? He was to be tormented for the rest of his days. The guilt should sit directly on his shoulders and he should suffer for it every day that he lived and breathed.

In that moment he knew he had to change his ways. He had to become a better person. He had to look out for others rather than only himself. He had to treasure his daughter and his friends. He could not continue to abuse them - abuse their trust and expect their forgiveness. He had to show them love and respect. He had to respect Fiona and let her get on with her life. She deserved way better. If he really loved her he had to let her go. For Mick that realisation cut very deep. He loved her like he had loved no other person on the planet. He always would. He had to settle down. His constant attempts to shag anything that moved were so wrong. He showed no respect to his conquests and in doing so showed no respect to himself. His moral standards were ridiculous. In that moment he knew he was going to change. He was about to enter a new phase of his life where he would earn the respect of his friends and his community. He was going to become a new man. He had been given another chance at life and he was about to grab it with both hands.

Toni leaned over the bed, her face close to his. She tried to reassure him that all was OK. She wiped the tears from his face and held his hand. As she tried to console him she realised he was in a totally different place - on a totally different planet. She sat by the bed and talked softly about nothing while Mick cried himself to sleep.

Post Script

Don't let the truth get in the way of a good story.

Two days after the deaths of George Richardson, Ben Flood and Beatrice Chowdry, ISIS claimed responsibility for the terrorist attack in Stewarts River, NSW, Australia.

World News reported by ABC, BBC, CNN, Al Jazeera et al. – Dr Rashid Chowdry had converted to Islam and become an ISIS sympathizer on numerous trips home to India in recent years. Chowdry had returned to Australia on a false passport to take revenge on Veterinarian Mick Gallagher. Gallagher had challenged ISIS to come and kill him after his father was murdered by the terrorist organisation in Jordan earlier this year. Chowdry murdered his wife as she could not be persuaded to convert to his beliefs.

When Julia Gallagher returned to Stewarts River and found out that Dr Adrian Harkin had saved her father's life on multiple occasions she rewarded him with way more than a hand job. Dr Harkin now plans on becoming a General Practitioner in Stewarts River.

Mr Adrian Bartholomew Llewellyn Smith a.k.a. "Smitho" was nominated by Stewarts River Council for the Order of Australia Medal in relation to his bravery and selfless behaviour on the day of the Stewarts River terrorist attack.

Mick Gallagher did not have sex for at least 2 weeks after being released from hospital.

23362642R00083

Printed in Great Britain
by Amazon